ELLA'S EMBRACE

Oregon Sky Book Three

KAY P. DAWSON

Ella's Embrace: Oregon Sky Book Three
Print version
© Copyright 2022 (As Revised) Kay P. Dawson

CKN Christian Publishing
An Imprint of Wolfpack Publishing
5130 S. Fort Apache Rd. 215-380
Las Vegas, NV 89148

cknchristianpublishing.com

Print ISBN 978-1-63977-225-4

ELLA'S EMBRACE

CHAPTER 1

"Thank you Walter, for giving a girl a chance to prove she could do more than look after a house. You taught me to ride, to break a horse, to care for animals and you never once made me feel like I couldn't do it. I'll never forget you." Ella's voice whispered the words as she reached down and placed a rose on the fresh ground where they'd just buried Walter Jenkins.

A sob escaped as she stood back up and she desperately fought to hold back the tears that were threatening again. She didn't think she had any left but it seemed there was an endless supply today.

She was sure the only time her heart had ever hurt this bad was when her own pa had died when she was just a girl of fifteen. Walter had filled that role for her after that, taking her under his wing when they arrived in Oregon and letting her fully develop her love for horses.

He'd painstakingly taught her everything he knew and had always let her believe she could do it. It didn't matter that she was a girl.

In his eyes, she could do anything.

She felt a hand on her shoulder and turned to see her younger brother, Logan, smiling at her. "You all right, sis?" His hand gave a gentle squeeze before he pulled it back.

All she could do was nod, afraid if she tried to speak she would break down again. Her brother must have sensed that. He took her hand and pulled her toward him, taking her in his arms for a hug. He was two years younger than her but he towered over her.

"You don't always have to pretend you're strong, Ella. Everyone knows how much you loved Walter. We all did. He's helped us all these years, making sure we got to Oregon on the wagon train after pa died, and then helping us set up and work our farm ever since, all the while he was setting up his own. He was a part of our family and it hurts to know he's gone."

Logan was the most sensitive of her brothers but she knew all of them were hurting too. Colton and Reid were sitting over under the tree with their wives but Connor had gone looking for gold down in California so he wasn't here today.

"I just can't believe it happened. Why did he have to be so stubborn? If he would've just listened, and let Titus go after the thief, none of this would've happened." Her words were muffled as she spoke into her brother's broad chest.

Someone had been stealing the best horses from Walter's farm for months, only taking one at a time and leaving long enough between thefts for everyone to start letting their guard down again. No one had been caught and there seemed to be no idea of who was doing it.

Well, except for some townsfolk who believed it was Henry Carson, the man who'd always wanted the land Walter homesteaded on. He'd been after Walter for years to sell to him and had even bought his own horses to try competing with him.

Along with farming his land, Walter had grown a nice herd of horses which he broke and trained to be bought by the cavalry around Oregon as well as new settlers moving into the area. He was becoming well known as the man to go to for horses.

"Because he was a stubborn old fool who couldn't listen." The sound of Titus's voice coming up behind her startled her, causing her to step back from her brother's arms and whirl to face him.

"He may have been stubborn but he wasn't a fool. I won't let you talk bad about him." She glared at the man in front of her.

She watched as Titus clenched his jaw. She could

see the muscles working as he tried to hold back his anger. Titus had been the one to find Walter, finally catching up to him after he'd raced out of the yard after the thief.

Even though he'd only been working with her and Walter on the farm for a few months now, Titus had seemed to have grown genuinely fond of the man. She knew it had upset him.

"Titus, I know you tried to stop him but when he got something in his head, you wouldn't have ever got him to listen to you." She tried to make him feel better, knowing he was carrying guilt over what happened that day.

Titus had been in the barn doing the early morning chores. Ella had just got there and the two of them had been arguing about something she couldn't even remember now. The truth was, she'd been arguing with Titus since the day he arrived in town and Walter had hired him.

The sound of a horse galloping past and Walter's voice yelling had brought them running outside, just in time to see Walter's back as he sped past the door of the barn.

"I've got you this time!" He'd been hollering after the figure on the horse that was just disappearing past the trees.

Titus had yelled at Walter to wait so he could follow too. But, Walter had insisted he wasn't letting the thief get away this time and kept riding.

By the time Titus had run back into the barn and grabbed one of the horses from the stalls, the other two riders were far out of view. Titus tore after them and as he rode out of the yard, they both heard the gunshot.

Ella would never forget the fear she had in her stomach, somehow knowing Walter wasn't coming back. She'd prayed Titus wasn't riding into the same fate but he hadn't even slowed down.

"Well, if I'd been in the yard like I was supposed to be, it would've been me going after the thief. Shouldn't have been Walter."

She tilted her head to one side. "So, in other words, it should've been you that was shot? And, instead, I'd be standing here listening to Walter saying it should've been him." She shook her head. "It doesn't matter anyway. What's done is done. It won't bring Walter back." Her voice choked as she finished her sentence.

Ella would never forget Titus coming back into the yard, carrying Walter on his horse. She'd never seen a man more upset than he was. He'd carried him into the house and laid him on his bed but they both knew he was already gone.

Titus had cursed and ran out the door, leaping back onto his horse to go after the coward who'd shot Walter. Of course, like always, the thief had disappeared without a trace.

"Ella, Titus, Mr. Harper wants to sit with us in

the house for a minute to discuss Walter's final wishes." Ella's mom, Anna, came over and put her arm around her daughter's shoulder as she led her back to the house.

The townsfolk were all starting to head back to town, leaving just her family, Titus and Mr. Harper, who was the only lawyer in the area, to discuss what would happen now. Walter's wife had died before he came west and, as far as they knew, there was no known kin besides a nephew, whom they had no clue how to contact.

Ella's heart broke to think that the farm and all of the horses she'd worked with would be sold. Her job working on the farm would be done. There weren't many other men who would hire a woman to help break horses.

She'd now be forced to rely on her family to support her unless, by some miracle, she could find a man to love her even though, at twenty-three, she was almost past marrying age. Not to mention the fact there weren't many men around these parts she'd be interested in marrying anyway.

And, she would never marry for anything less than love.

They all sat around the empty table in the small house Walter had built when he arrived in Oregon. His house was sparse, most of his money and time had been invested in the barns where he kept his animals.

"Now that I have you all here, I wanted to make sure we have a chance to go over everything Walter had written down as his final wishes. He'd been in to see me a few times to make sure everything was in order if anything should happen to him. He knew he wasn't a young man anymore." Mr. Harper was a small man with wire-rimmed glasses who was always nervous around Ella or any other woman for that matter. She watched him now as he shuffled papers and swallowed hard, unable to look anyone in the room in the eye.

"What will happen to the farm and all of the animals now, Mr. Harper? Walter had one nephew who'd lived with him for a while but he died when he had fallen off his horse, not too long ago. He'd mentioned another nephew he has back east but said he hadn't spoken with him in a while." Ella kept her eyes on Mr. Harper, who wouldn't look up at her.

"Well, um, yes. There is a nephew." He shifted uncomfortably and looked around the room at the men, landing his gaze on Titus.

Mr. Harper pulled at his collar. "Walter didn't have much besides what's here on this farm. And, he's left all of that to the two of you." He nodded his head toward Titus, then her.

"What? Why?" Ella was dumbfounded. Walter left his land and animals to her?

And Titus?

7

"He loved you like a granddaughter, he told me that on more than one occasion. He left me a letter to give you if anything ever happened to him. He wrote it over a year ago." He reached into the pile of papers and pulled out an envelope and she immediately recognized Walter's scribbled print.

Her hands trembled as she took it from his hands, then stood to go to the far side of the small room. She didn't want the others to watch her read it.

Unfolding the paper, she sat down in the small chair Walter had always sat in by the fireplace and looked down at the paper through eyes already blurred from tears.

Dearest Ella,

I guess if you are reading this, then I've gone to be with my dear Mary. You know I'm not much for words, but I thought I should tell you what I hadn't been able to in life. You meant an awful lot to me, Ella, how you came and helped me on my farm, helping an old man keep living the life he dreamed of. You may not have been blood kin but, to me, you were the dearest child I could have asked for.

I want you to keep living your dream, and I hope you'll keep things going for me when I'm gone. I know things are tough as a woman, and owning some land of your own might ease some of the worries I know you have.

You might not be too happy when you hear I'm also going to be leaving the rest to my nephew back east. But, I know you, and I know you'll be able to handle him. He can be a bit difficult, but he's an honorable man. He carries his own burdens and I'd like to believe you could see the good in him.

So, dear Ella, I will leave the horses you loved, and the farm you helped me care for, in your hands. I know you'll take care of it all for me.

And, my nephew, Titus, will help you, if you let him.

Until we meet again,
Walter

Her head started spinning as she finished reading the words on the paper.

Titus? She lifted her eyes and found him staring at her from the chair he was sitting in. Everyone else was sitting quietly, watching to see what the letter had said.

There's no way it could be a coincidence his name was the same as Walter's nephew. And, the look in his eyes as he watched her, told her he knew he'd just been found out.

Her entire body shook as she realized she'd been lied to for the past few months, by both Walter and the man in front of her.

He was more than just a hired hand who'd found a job with Walter.

"Why didn't you tell us you were Walter Jenkins' nephew?"

CHAPTER 2

"So, Titus, do you want to fill us in on what exactly is going on? You've never given us an honest answer about why you're here or why you felt the need to lie about who you are. And, before you think we're going to let our sister be stuck in some kind of forced partnership with you without finding out what the deal is, you're even crazier than you look."

Titus cringed at the sound of Colton's voice behind him. He'd been standing quietly, enjoying a piece of pie beside a tree in the yard and had hoped no one would pay him any mind.

He wasn't even sure why he'd agreed to come out to Colton and Phoebe's after church today. But, when Anna Wallace, the matriarch of the family, invited him, he'd found himself saying yes before he could stop himself.

He supposed it was a bit lonely with his uncle gone – the fact that Ella still wasn't talking to him unless she absolutely had to when they were working on the horses, he was likely missing human contact.

Walter had only been gone a few days and Ella still came out every day to work on the farm, so he guessed it wasn't like he was entirely alone.

He sighed. "I reckon if you think back real hard Colton, you'll realize I never did lie about who I am. No one ever asked, so I didn't feel inclined to tell."

He put another piece of pie in his mouth, savoring the flavor. He wasn't much of a cook and Walter hadn't been either, so he hadn't tasted anything quite this good in some time.

Colton moved around in front of him and Titus noticed Logan, the younger brother, move to the other side of him. He let his eyes move around the yard until he found Reid sitting under a tree with his wife. He wondered why he wasn't over here on the attack too.

"You mean to tell me, all the way back when you joined that wagon train in Missouri to come out to Oregon, you never thought to mention that you had an uncle here in Bethany? Not even any of the times I talked about coming back home to the exact same location?"

Titus had joined a wagon train headed west when he decided to come west to find his brother's killer. It just so happened, Colton had been the man leading that outfit.

Titus would admit he might have been a bit arrogant and cocky, causing him and Colton to butt heads on more than one occasion. However, the anger and guilt he'd been carrying at the time had left him feeling numb to anything but revenge for his brother.

He hadn't told Colton because he'd already decided he was going to find who killed his brother, without anyone knowing who he was. He didn't need anyone else knowing the truth. And, at the time, he still didn't know who he could trust.

But, he knew he needed to tell all of Ella's family the truth now. She was standing beside Logan, obviously intent on hearing what he had to say. He couldn't help notice how beautiful she looked when she was wearing proper woman's clothes.

"Listen, I've already spoke to Mr. Harper and was going to tell you all anyway. You don't need to form a posse to beat the information out of me. Since your family was close with my uncle, and especially now that I'm partners with your *charming* sister, you may as well know the truth." He noticed the scowl she gave him after his sideways glance and raised eyebrow at the mention of her personality trait.

"But, what I tell you here is only for your ears. My uncle and I went to a great deal of trouble to keep my identity hidden from everyone around these parts. And now, as far as anyone else knows, he had no kin and the farm was left entirely to Ella. I'm just staying to help for a while."

"Why don't you want anyone to know Walter was your uncle?" Logan was looking at Titus like he'd grown another head, unsure why he'd bother to lie about any of this.

"Because after my brother Martin was killed when he came out to help him, we decided not to give the thief anyone else to go after. We figured if everyone assumed he had no more kin, whoever was doing this would let their guard down a bit and slip up so we could catch him."

His heart clenched at the mention of his brother. Martin had been only a year younger than him and been so full of happiness and life even after the years of living with their father had nearly destroyed them both.

"I thought Martin fell off his horse and hit his head? That's what Walter told us. We never knew he'd been killed." Reid had walked up behind them now, obviously realizing there was a conversation going on he needed to be in on.

That's what everyone had thought. But when Walter had written to him with the news, they'd both known that wasn't the whole story. The extra set of prints near the horse when Walter found him had left no doubt that Martin hadn't simply fallen and hit his head.

"My brother was an excellent horseman. He wouldn't have fallen from a horse. There was more to it than that."

He pushed himself off from the tree he'd been leaning on and moved to look out over the small creek running past the property. They could hear Reid's daughter, Sophia, laughing as she played with Phoebe and Audrey, and the voices of James and Susan O'Hara were lifted in discussion with Anna.

But the people standing around, listening to Titus, remained silent as they waited for him to continue.

"My uncle wrote us a few years ago, saying he wanted us to come out and learn the ropes so he could pass on his farm to us. He was my grandmother's youngest brother and he and my aunt Mary never had children of their own. They'd raised my mother after her parents died, so had thought of her as their own."

He smiled as he remembered his mother's face.

"After Walter's wife passed away, he wanted a new start away from there. He sold what he could, packed up the rest and headed west. He'd been out here for a couple of years when he sent back for us to come out. By then, my ma had passed and, of course, my father wouldn't allow it. But Walter never gave up trying. The last time he mailed us, my brother decided he was going to come west to follow his dreams and live with Walter."

"Around the time my brother arrived, someone had started stealing horses from my uncle and Martin was determined to find out who was doing it. The last letter he sent me said he'd finally found some evidence after the last theft. A piece from an envelope with an address from Oregon City was left on the ground where the horse had been stolen from. He'd given me the name on the paper and said he was going to confront the man."

He could feel the muscles in his body tightening as he relived everything.

"He never made it back to my uncle's. And, he'd never told Walter anything because he didn't want him to get hurt. Any of the information my brother had he took to his grave with him." He cursed under his breath then turned back to face them.

"I knew I should've come out with him. My reasons for wanting to stay home shouldn't have been more important. When he was sending me letters telling me what was going on out here, I should've come. He died trying to defend my uncle's land and I wasn't here to help."

He turned to Colton. "After he died, I packed up everything I had to come here and find out who did it. When I heard there was a wagon train heading west, I had to join. I know I may have been a bit hard to deal with along the way but you need to understand the anger I was trying to deal with. I was furious at whoever killed my brother but I was even more angry at myself. He was my little brother and I should've been there to help him."

Colton's blue eyes stared at him before he gave a nod. "I would've been the same. No need to explain."

"I stayed in Oregon City when we arrived to talk to the man my brother had been to see. Realizing it had been a false lead, I then headed out here to find the thief myself. Walter and I both decided it best to let everyone keep believing I was nothing more than a hired hand. We didn't want the thief to know I would have any vested interest in helping to catch him. And, since it's obvious whoever is doing this wants the land, or at the least to put Walter out of business, we thought it best just to leave our family relationship between us."

None of the men around him were moving. They all stood completely still and he found his eyes moving to Ella. The blue eyes were locked on his face and she was twisting her hands in front of her as though she weren't quite sure what to do with them.

He figured she preferred being angry at him and hearing him explain why he'd done what he had was causing her some confusion.

Turning his head to look at each of the Wallace brothers standing in front of him, he continued. "I'd like to keep it that way. As far as anyone knows, Walter's farm went entirely to Ella with no kin to pass it down to. Mr. Harper has ensured me no one else will learn the truth. I hope it will bring the thief out of hiding thinking it will be easy to get now."

He paused as he tried to figure out how to tell them the rest of his plan without them all throwing him to the ground and pummeling him.

"Since everyone assumes Ella is the sole heir, she needs to move out to the farm."

He waited for the gasps from Ella and the hollering from the brothers he knew he was about to hear. He was fully aware of the absurdity of his plan but it was all he had. The past couple of days had left him with time to think and he knew it was the only way.

"Are you crazy? You want us to let our sister move out to Walter's, with you, while someone is willing to kill whoever gets in their way to get this land?" Logan was usually more reserved, so Titus was a bit surprised the first argument hadn't come from Colton or Reid.

Titus turned his head and watched her. He'd known her long enough now to see that she was already thinking it over. He needed to appeal to her. "I need to catch the man responsible for killing my brother and my uncle. I owe it to them. For some reason, whoever is doing this wants what we have and I need them to think they're close to getting it. If Ella doesn't move out there, they'll wonder why. I doubt she'll be in danger. The thief will believe she's going to be easy to get the land from, without having to hurt her, since she's a woman on her own." Ella scowled at him when he said that last bit. He knew she wouldn't be able to resist proving everyone wrong.

"No, she's not staying out there. It's too danger-ous. Not to mention the damage to her reputation as a single woman living out there with the likes of you." Reid was shaking his head, already decided it wasn't going to happen.

"There are plenty of women who have to take on hired help after their husband dies in order to keep their farms going to provide for their families. This is no different." He tried to reason with them.

"It's plenty different and you know it. Ella isn't a widow. She's an unmarried woman who'd be living out there with a man who isn't her husband." Logan wasn't backing down either.

"I'll sleep in the barn. Ella will have the house all to herself."

"I'm going to do it."

Her voice was so quiet the brothers just kept talking, not even paying any attention to her. But Titus had heard and he knew she'd make sure her brothers eventually heard her too.

"I don't even like her working out there with

you now that Walter isn't around. It's only a matter of time until people start talking." Colton was shaking his head too.

"I said, I'm going to do it."

Her voice was louder this time, finally breaking into the conversation between the men.

"I loved Walter like a grandfather. I owe this to him. I want to catch whoever killed him, and the best way to do that is to be out there." She put her hand up in the air as Logan moved forward to argue with her.

"No, I've made up my mind. And besides, my reputation doesn't matter much around these parts. In everyone's opinion, I'm already past marrying age anyway. I'm a big girl and I can make my own decisions." She turned to face Titus directly. Somehow, he'd known she'd do this regardless of what everyone else thought.

"I need to do this for Walter."

CHAPTER 3

E lla let the horse have its lead, crouching low behind the mare's neck and holding tight to the reins. The horse she was riding today was just about the best-trained horse she'd ever worked with. Walter had let her name it and she'd decided to call her Storm. She'd been found with some others in her herd during a winter snowstorm and Ella instantly fell in love with her.

She was going to have a hard time selling Storm but she knew she was almost ready to go. For now though, she could enjoy the feel of the wind blowing her hair out behind her as the horse ran across the open field. The sound of the hooves pounding the ground matched her heart beat and she closed her eyes as she let the horse lead the way.

Her heart ached for the man who'd given her the chance to grow her love for these horses. She missed him terribly and she knew she'd give up everything he'd left her in a heartbeat if it'd bring him back.

Opening her eyes, she could see the gap in the trees where she could let Storm drink from the creek. Hopping down from the mare's back, she led her over to the water then went and leaned back against the tree she always found herself under when she needed time alone.

She sat quietly, letting the sounds of the trickling water and birds singing in the trees around her bring her comfort. Alone, she could let her grief take over and her tears could fall freely.

The past few days had taken their toll on her. After deciding she'd move out to Walter's small shack, she'd faced arguments from her entire family. She knew it wasn't "proper" to be out on a secluded ranch with a man she wasn't wedded to. It didn't matter that Titus had moved out to the barn so she could have the house to herself. Her reputation would most likely be damaged but she didn't care.

Besides the fact she'd do anything to find out who'd done this to Walter after everything he'd done for her, the truth was, she'd long given up hope of finding love and marrying. Out here in Oregon, there were plenty of men for her to choose from but there were none who made her heart flutter.

She knew it was silly but she always remembered

her mom telling her the stories of when she'd met her pa.

That's what Ella wanted.

It wasn't that there hadn't been many opportunities to find herself a husband. Many men had made their intentions known but she hadn't found one who gave her that feeling. And now, it was well known around the area that she was past marrying age and people talked, saying she wouldn't be interested anyway.

Maybe she should have just married one of the men who'd paid her attention when she had the chance. Maybe love wasn't going to happen for her. She wanted her own home and her own family and, as much as she pretended it didn't bother her, she longed for someone to care for her.

Everyone knew she was independent and headstrong and they assumed she didn't care if she ever married.

But, she didn't want to be a burden on her family. She didn't want to be the old spinster that had no one. She wanted a house, she wanted children, and she wanted a man who loved her.

She'd always believed it would happen if she just gave it time. Now she worried that her time had passed and she would be alone. At least Walter had made sure she'd have some independence. The thought of him doing that for her brought more tears to her eyes.

A noise in the bush caused her to sit up straight, and the mare lifted her head from her drink and flitted her ears in the same direction. As she looked in the direction of the noise, she could see the bushes move and through the branches came the sorriest looking animal she'd ever seen.

It limped over to the water and Storm moved closer to sniff at it. It resembled a horse but Ella could tell by its ears and some other features it was most likely a mule.

Not wanting to scare it off, she moved up onto her knees, then slowly stood, moving closer to the animal that was now bending its head down for water, not seeming to care that the big mare beside it was sniffing her.

Before she could get any closer, Titus came charging through the opening in the trees, startling them all. She'd been so intent on getting to the mule, she hadn't even heard him coming.

The mule tried to run but was obviously in such rough shape it couldn't move fast enough to get far. She turned and glared at Titus who wasn't even paying attention as he dismounted. He strode over to her, letting go of his horse's lead so it could get some water.

"Did you seriously need to come charging in here like the devil was on your heels?" She crossed her arms in front of her for extra effect.

He stopped and creased his eyebrows as he

looked at her. "Beg your pardon?"

She flipped her hand in the direction of the poor mule that was now standing to the side of the bush with its head hanging down as though it were defeated. Its sides heaved with exhaustion.

Titus tipped his head to get a better look at it past her, then started to slowly walk toward it.

"Hey there, old girl. I'm not gonna hurt you." His voice was low and steady as he crept closer to the mule who was now watching him warily.

When he got closer, he put his hand out to let it smell his glove.

"Hand me the rope off my saddle." He didn't even turn back to her as he kept his eyes on the mule. She walked over to his horse and pulled the rope off the saddle, then carefully walked over to him.

"Where do you think she came from?" She kept her voice in a whisper as she handed him the rope. He quickly knotted it and looped it around the animal's neck. It didn't even move, keeping its eyes on Titus. It was almost as though there was no fight left in it anyway, so it was ready to see what they were going to do.

"I reckon she's come out on a wagon train and been left after she couldn't go on perhaps. She looks in pretty rough shape." He leaned down and looked at the mule's sides, rubbing his hands over the ribs that were showing. He shook his head.

"Lots of sores and I'd say she's hurt her hind leg. Likely why she was left behind to fend for herself."

"Well, that's horrible! Who would do such a thing?" Ella couldn't believe anyone would be so cruel.

Titus lifted his head and peeked at her from under his hat. "You work with horses. You know what happens when they come lame. Sometimes it's just what needs to be done."

"No, Titus, that's not how *I* do things. So, we are taking this poor animal back to the farm and we're going to nurse her back to health." She was already walking back to her own horse.

She ignored the look she noticed him give her before she turned around.

"Ella, this mule isn't going to live much longer. She's in a bad way and I'm afraid to say, she likely won't even make the trip back to the farm." Titus pulled on the rope, anyway, coaxing the animal forward.

"I'm not leaving it here, Titus. Even if I have to put it up on my horse with me, it's coming with us."

She was facing him, with her arms crossed in front of her. He cursed quietly under his breath but it was loud enough she could make out what he said. She instantly felt her cheeks warm at his language.

"Well, don't expect me to be caring for it. I have my own work I need to be doing." He was grumbling as he took the reins of his horse in his other hand, while she led hers out of the brush and back into the field that led to the farm.

"What were you doing coming out here anyway?" She looked sideways at him as they started walking back home.

Home. It felt strange to be saying that about Walter's and it was even more odd to know she was going there with a man who wasn't her husband.

She still wasn't sure how she felt about Titus. He frustrated her just about all the time but they seemed to have a comfortable understanding knowing they were doing this for Walter. He was ornery and bossy but he didn't seem to be someone she had to fear.

"I saw you riding hell bent across the field and then you disappeared, so I thought I better check on you."

It was her turn to look at him with an eyebrow raised in surprise. "You were worried about me?"

He gave a low chuckle, never even looking in her direction.

"You were riding a horse that's going to bring us a tidy profit. So I reckon I was worried."

She rolled her eyes. Of course, he'd be worried about the horse.

They walked in silence for a while, with the sounds of the animal's hooves that were trailing behind and the grunting of the mule, reaching their ears.

"So, how come you never married?"

She almost tripped over her own feet at the sudden question. She squinted her eyes in anger as she looked his direction.

"Has no one ever told you it isn't polite to ask a lady personal questions?"

He just shrugged and kept walking. "I figure since we're now business partners, I should try to find out more about you." He looked her direction. "I find it hard to believe no man has ever tried for your hand when women in these parts are so scarce."

She couldn't believe he was asking her these questions.

"Well, not that it's any of your business but, yes, there have been men who've tried for my affections but none who I felt were suited." That's all he needed to know.

The sound of laughter deep in his throat caused her teeth to clench.

"What would make a man suited to you?"

"Well, first of all, he'd have to be kind and not abrasive and rude." She shot a glare in his direction to let him know she was talking about his own personality. "And, he would have to be able to make me laugh and be willing to let me work alongside him without making me feel like I wasn't capable because I'm a woman. But, the most important thing would be that he'd have to make my heart feel like it was going to flip right out of my chest when he was near me and, when I looked in his eyes, I would know he loved me."

Titus stopped and turned to face her, letting his horse and the mule take a rest.

"You're not asking for much," Titus said sarcastically and shook his head. "Only love I ever seen like that was my uncle Walter and my aunt Mary. He looked at her that way. But, that's a rare thing from what I've seen." He started walking again.

"So, why aren't you married?" She figured if he thought he could ask her personal questions, then so could she.

She saw him shake his head as he gave a little laugh. "Oh trust me, I ain't the marrying kind. No woman would want to be saddled with me."

"I'm sure even someone as grumpy as you could find a woman who could put up with you."

She knew most men didn't think they wanted to get married until they had to live a while with no one to make them decent meals or to care for their homes. She wondered why he seemed so adamant about not marrying. She waited for him to reply as they finally walked into the yard, the poor mule almost ready to collapse. She'd almost forgot what they were talking about it took him so long to continue.

"I would never marry a woman and risk becoming like my father."

CHAPTER 4

He came into the yard after working the field all day, ready to collapse in his makeshift bed in the barn. The fact that he was sleeping in that close proximity to a mule was a bit of a sore spot with him but Ella had insisted the flea-ridden thing needed the best care.

And, that meant he slept in the barn with it.

She hadn't appreciated his thoughts on naming the animal Ella since he figured their personalities matched nicely. However, after realizing upon further inspection it was in fact a male, they'd agreed to call it Wally, after his uncle who'd also been as stubborn as a mule.

He shook his head as he thought about how much his life had turned since arriving in Oregon. Growing up in Tennessee, he'd always helped on the family farm while Walter was living there. He loved farming and he loved working with the animals too. When his uncle had still lived there with his aunt Mary, times had been happy.

However, eventually, his father decided to sell the portion of the farm Walter had deeded to his mom on her marriage. His father had wanted riches and farming wasn't going to bring him that. He needed money to start a business, so he'd gambled the money he got for the farm, hoping for a windfall.

Instead, he'd lost it all. They spent the rest of the years struggling. Titus's mother took on jobs cleaning and doing people's laundry to survive while his father took up drinking.

Titus hated his father. He'd always been a cruel man. When Walter had moved to Oregon, he'd sent a letter back trying to get his mother to leave and bring the kids to live with him. When his father had found the letter, he'd beaten her so badly she'd barely been recognizable.

After that, his mother just gave up, going into a shell where she could escape from the reality that was her life. When she got pneumonia one winter, she had no fight in her to survive.

With a brother and sister to care for, Titus had spent the rest of his days there, trying to keep them safe from their father as he tried his best to keep them from starving.

He'd been happy when Martin finally moved out

to Oregon but Titus had stayed to make sure his sister was safe. She'd married shortly before Martin was killed, so he'd known it was finally safe to leave.

He hadn't spoken to his father since and, as far as he knew, the man may have finally drank himself to death.

He'd always planned to head back home after he'd helped his uncle and found his brother's killer. He wasn't sure why other than that was all he knew as home.

But, as he looked around the fields and took in the beauty of the land around him, he wasn't sure how he could leave here now. He didn't even know where home was anymore.

Of course, he still had the problem of a partner who seemed more than happy when he'd told her he wouldn't be sticking around long. How would things work if he did decide to stay?

He saw the woman he was thinking about outside banging a dusty mat on a rock. She'd spent the past few days trying to bring Walter's old shack up to standards for a woman to live in before she moved out here for good but he knew she was likely no closer than she was when she started.

"There won't be any fabric left to that old thing if you keep banging it like that." He stopped the team he was leading with the plow and turned to unhitch them.

She barely acknowledged him as she turned and

carried the rug back inside. His nose caught a whiff of something that smelled like heaven as his stomach started to grumble with hunger. He let the horses go, then followed the scent.

He stood in the open doorway and looked around in shock. The shack had been completely transformed into a livable space. She'd obviously cleaned everything top to bottom and the bed in the corner had a flowery quilt on it he didn't recognize. There was a pot hanging over the fire and the aroma in the room had him drooling.

He let out a whistle. "You've been busy." He let his gaze take in everything in the room. His eyes landed on a trunk in the corner. "You've brought your things out?" He glanced in her direction.

"Yes, Logan brought the wagon out with everything I needed earlier when you were in the field. I figured it was as clean as it was going to get in here, so there was no sense putting off moving out here any longer." She was busy stirring whatever was in the pot, so didn't even turn around.

He was sure his stomach was being louder than a herd of stampeding buffaloes but they hadn't ever really discussed how things would work once she was living here permanently. He assumed he'd be taking his own meals that he'd make himself over a fire by the barn. He was sure he wouldn't be welcome traipsing in and out of her house now that it wasn't Walter's.

The old cot he'd slept on when his uncle had been alive had already been moved out to the barn, so that would be his home now until other arrangements could be figured out.

Besides, maybe she wouldn't even want to stay out here once the thief was caught. She could continue coming out to work, if that's what she decided, but she wouldn't have to be stuck living on the farm with her partner in a shack that wasn't suitable for a lady to live in.

Whatever the plan would be, at the moment, he didn't care. The smell coming from that pot had his thoughts consumed.

"Something smells good." He hoped he didn't sound too desperate to eat whatever it was.

She turned and moved over to the small cupboard that had a few plates. "Well, if you'd get cleaned up and sit down, I can get you a bowl."

He nodded coolly, not wanting to give away how much he'd hoped she would offer.

Hanging his hat on the hook, he walked over to the bowl that had fresh water in it. He wasn't quite sure if he was supposed to use the fancy soap sitting beside it, knowing he would leave it as black as his hands if he did. She must have noticed his hesitation as he heard her give a little laugh. "You can use the soap. We usually make our own, which isn't quite as fancy, but this was one I'd picked up at the mercantile in town one time and never used."

He tried to ignore the flowery smell on his hands as he went back to the table.

"I figure since I can't help much in the fields doing the work, the least I could do is make sure you're fed well." She set a bowl of stew in front of him, then turned to grab a basket of freshly made buns to set on the table. He hadn't eaten this well in a long time.

When Walter had been alive, they'd normally just eat some bread and bacon which seemed to be Walter's specialty.

She sat across the table from him and he wasn't quite sure if he was supposed to wait for her to start eating or what the proper manner was. She bowed her head and started saying grace, so he was glad he hadn't started spooning the stew into his mouth.

He looked at the top of her head as it was bowed quietly in prayer. He knew her and Colton were twins, yet her hair was so blonde compared to his dark hair. But, they both had the bright blue eyes that it seemed the entire Wallace family had. Those eyes lifted and met his across the table as he sat holding his spoon full of food ready to eat.

He almost felt his eyes close as he took the first bite. He knew she was still watching him, and he didn't want to let on that he was enjoying it as much as he was, so he just nodded his head in her direction. "Good stew." He lifted another spoonful to his mouth.

"My ma has spent a lot of time teaching me to cook for when I get married." She gave a little laugh, then rolled her eyes. "But, mostly I just learned so I could help her with the cooking for our family. With all of my brothers at home, it was hard to keep up with the amount of food they were eating sometimes."

She picked nervously at her own food in front of her and he could tell by the way she kept glancing up at him that she wanted to talk about something else.

"Garett Jackson was over today." She kept her eyes on him as he used a piece of the bun to sop up the gravy. "He arrived just after Logan and I pulled in with the wagon. He saw me bringing my things in."

He wasn't sure why she was just sitting and staring at him as though what she was telling him was supposed to mean something.

Finally finishing the bowl off, he leaned back to give her his attention before asking for another helping.

"What did he want?" Garett Jackson farmed the land beside them and had been a help to his uncle over the years. He was older than Titus, closer to his forties, but he'd never married. Titus wasn't sure what had Ella so concerned about his visit.

She spun her spoon around in her fingers, still avoiding looking at him.

"He was just coming to pay his respects and to see if I needed a hand around here." She finally met his gaze. "He was shocked to see me moving into the house, especially when I mentioned you'd be staying on to help too."

He shrugged. "We knew people were going to talk. Not much we can do about that. People will be inclined to believe what they want regardless of what we tell them, so no sense worrying about it."

She sat with her mouth half open staring at him. "Of course a man would say that. I know I said I didn't care what people said about my reputation but I didn't think it would be starting already."

He watched her as she stood to get more stew out of the pot and put it into his bowl. "It's just that...I don't know. I know my chances of finding a husband are pretty low anyway but I guess deep down I still held onto the hope that some man would be able to see me for who I am and could possibly love me. Now I know it likely won't happen, so I guess it's just going to take some getting used to." She set the bowl in front of him then went back to start cleaning up around the kitchen. She bent down and lifted a pail of water to boil so she could do some dishes. He noticed it was full, so she had to have gone down to the creek herself to fill it.

Most women wouldn't have done that and would've waited for the man to come in and do it.

But, he was quickly learning Ella wasn't like most women.

"Well, I guess I could marry you. That would solve your problems."

Where had that come from? He had a fairly good idea how much she would like that idea, and she wasn't long confirming it.

"I won't have any man marry me out of pity or because he feels obligated. I told you before, I will only marry for love." She turned and put her hands on her hips and he had to fight to keep from grinning. "And anyway, I'd rather die an old lonely spinster than ever be tied for life to someone like you!"

He was happy to see the Ella he'd come to know over the past few weeks come back out. He knew Walter's death had thrown her for a loop and she was having a hard time adjusting to everything. But, he much preferred the girl who wasn't afraid to tell him exactly what she was thinking.

"Oh but my dear, we're already tied together for life. We have a farm together or did you forget that?"

He watched as she clenched her fists at her sides. "I thought you said after we caught the thief, you were fine with just walking away and letting me take over?" Her eyes squinted at him suspiciously.

"I did. But, I've been thinking about how much I like it here and I reckon, with enough persuasion, I just might stay."

He stood up and grabbed his hat from the hook, tipping it down towards her before walking out the door. He smiled to himself as he saw her mouth tighten into a fine line and her hands ball even further into fists.

Even though he didn't plan on staying, he was enjoying making her believe he was.

CHAPTER 5

Wally pushed against her with his nose, hoping for another carrot. The mule was feeling better but was still walking with a limp. He wasn't the nicest looking animal she'd ever seen but there was something about the creature that just made her happy.

He was already fiercely loyal to her, following her everywhere when she was in the yard. And, even after everything it had gone through, it hadn't given up. It seemed to know it was safe here and Ella was sure the animal even smiled at her sometimes when she looked at it.

She was getting the animals all ready for the night, doing the final chores, while Titus finished setting out some hay. For two people who were forced into an unusual partnership like this one, they'd adapted fairly well. She guessed since they'd already been working on the farm for a few months anyway, it wasn't too hard to adjust.

The only thing that really was different now was Titus having to do the work that Walter would have done too and, of course, the fact that she was going to be living here with him. Well, not really with him but on the same property. In the eyes of many people, they were already living in sin.

At least she had the support of her family and the close friends who lived in the area. Everyone who knew her knew she was doing this for Walter and to take care of the gift of independence he'd given her by leaving her his farm.

There were others in town who couldn't figure out why she didn't just sell it. A woman trying to farm land and train horses on her own wasn't something people were used to seeing. A few people had even questioned if she would legally be entitled to own the land since she was a woman.

But, they didn't realize that Titus also had ownership.

She looked out across the fields at the sun setting behind the hills. The sounds of the animals around her, along with the crickets that were starting to sing their nightly chorus, was music to her ears. She loved this place and was so grateful for the chance to prove she could take care of it. There weren't many women who independently owned land and she vowed to do everything she could to make Walter proud.

The sound of Titus grumbling at Wally as the mule walked over and poked in his pockets for a treat reached her ears, causing her to turn and watch them. She smiled to herself because even though Titus tried to let on to everyone around him that he was gruff and didn't care about much, she'd gotten to see a different side of him over the past few weeks of working with him. And, even more so since Walter had died.

There weren't many men who would accept a woman as partner especially when he could have fought the will and said, since he was the only kin, he was entitled to all of it.

But, he never did and he'd let her keep working as she always had, without ever questioning whether or not she could do something because she was a woman.

She wasn't sure why he tried to keep people at a distance but she guessed he had his reasons. At least they seemed to work together well, most of the time. When he wasn't trying to start an argument just for something to do, or annoy her, they got along quite nicely.

The truth was, if he hadn't already been so clear about his feelings about marriage and about the fact he wasn't sticking around after the thief was caught, she might be willing to admit she felt a strange attraction to him.

She wasn't quite sure what it was. She knew for a fact it wasn't love because she saw how her sisters-in-law looked at her brothers with eyes that left nothing to the imagination. And, they looked back at them with adoration.

The only way Titus ever seemed to look at her was with an eyebrow raised while shaking his head in frustration.

His brown hair had grown since he'd arrived and he never seemed to be completely shaved. She'd seen him a few times with his shirt undone and she felt herself flush as she remembered the muscles she'd seen moving as he worked.

"Ella, will you get Wally and pen him up for the night? Unless he's sleeping with you in the house, you better get him locked up in the barn. He wouldn't be able to outrun any animals who might wander in looking for a late night snack." His voice sounded annoyed.

Wasn't he feeling uncomfortable at all knowing this would be her first night actually staying at the farm alone with him?

The yard wasn't big. It had a chicken coop to one side of the house and a fenced-off area on the other side that she used to work with the horses. There were smaller pens around the yard that had a few of the horses locked in and another smaller barn that held some cattle for milking.

The main barn was across from the house but still close enough that she was feeling nervous at being in such close proximity with a man all night.

"And, the blasted animal better keep quiet tonight or I'll be locking him out myself." He had been complaining for the past couple of days about Wally's noise at night. But, Ella figured since Wally hadn't been feeling well, it was likely the reason.

Walking over and scratching behind the mule's ears, she looked at the animal's face. "Oh poor Wally. Is grumpy old Titus giving you bad dreams at night? Just ignore him and try to get some sleep." She was still smiling when she backed up and looked over at Titus.

He was standing leaning against a shovel in his hand as he looked at her. "Very funny, Ella. I'm serious. You have no idea what it's like sleeping beside this flea-bitten animal."

"Well, you could lock him in one of the stalls you know." She knew exactly why Wally wasn't locked in a stall, instead choosing to sleep right beside the cot Titus had been sleeping on. The first night, the animal had made such a ruckus, Titus had to let it out to sleep near him. And, the same had happened last night, so she was sure it was likely going to be a regular occurrence.

After getting the animal in the barn, she walked

back outside, stopping short when she saw Titus standing on the other side of the door with his shirt off, pouring water on himself. He hadn't seen her yet, with his back to her, and she didn't know which way to look. He had a cloth and was pulling it over his face, before dipping it back into the cool water in a pail he had sitting beside him.

She hadn't really thought about what he'd do for washing or anything like that but she guessed he'd already figured it all out. She felt bad staring at him but the muscles in his back moving as he washed had her senses doing strange things.

He turned and looked at her, holding the cloth out in front of him. "Would you mind washing my back instead of just standing there watching?" The grin on his face caused her cheeks to burn and she pushed past him as fast as her legs would take her.

She could hear him chuckling as she made her way to the house.

"G'night Ella."

She wasn't even going to give him the satisfaction of a reply.

☙❧

THE NIGHT WAS hot and no matter how much she tossed and turned, she couldn't get to sleep. The sight of Titus standing without his shirt was stuck in her mind and she couldn't seem to stop thinking about it.

What was wrong with her? She'd grown up with four brothers, so had seen many men without shirts in her lifetime, and Titus was no different.

But, she had to admit, she saw something entirely different when she'd seen him.

Sitting up, she swung her legs over the edge of the bed. She leaned her arms on her legs, letting the breeze from the open window hit her face. Her nightgown flowed loosely around her as she stood up and stretched. It felt so strange sleeping in a bed she wasn't used to but as she looked around the tiny house that was all in this one room, she felt a tug in her heart knowing Walter had believed in her enough to leave this for her.

It may not be much but it was hers. And, it might be all she would ever have of her own, so she would treasure it with everything she had.

Hearing a noise outside the window, she moved the frayed curtain aside to peek out. It was too dark to see anything, so she went to the door. She smiled to herself as she thought it was most likely Wally causing a ruckus and waking Titus up.

She walked out onto the small porch on the front of the house and breathed in the fresh air around her. Even though it was dark, the light from the moon showed the outlines of the buildings and the animals in the pens. She sat on the step, pulling her legs up tight beneath her in her nightgown and hugged them.

The night closed around her, holding her in darkness, and the only sounds she could hear were the stomping of an animal and the singing of the frogs down by the creek.

Suddenly, a flicker of light caught her eye over by the barn. Looking over, she expected to see Titus walking out with the lantern but she couldn't see him anywhere.

Staring in horror, she suddenly realized the barn was on fire.

She leaped to her feet, running across the ground to the door of the barn. She threw the door open and was almost pushed back with the smoke and flames that were already reaching out to touch her.

"Titus!" She coughed through the smoke, waving her hands in front of her face to try and clear the sight so she could see better. She reached to unlatch the stall for the first horse by the door, slapping it on the back to get it out outside.

Where was Titus?

"Get the hell out of here Ella! I've got it!" She heard his voice and could just make out his silhouette as he tugged on the rope around Wally's head. The animal was terrified and was pulling back, making it difficult to move him.

"Here, let me take him while you get the other

stalls opened up." She reached for the rope and Wally must have sensed that she was going to make things better. He went into a full run to stay with her.

She glanced back over her shoulder and saw Titus heading back through the flames. A board fell from the roof, and narrowly missed hitting him, but he kept going further in. She couldn't leave him in there on his own. There were still at least five horses in that barn and he wasn't going to be able to get them all out by himself.

Leaving Wally standing outside where it was safe, she ran back in. She could see Storm pawing at the ground in her stall and she ran to open the latch for her to get out. One of the other horses ran past her almost knocking her to the ground.

Just as she unhitched the latch to Storm's stall, she saw something out of the corner of her eye and realized that something was coming toward her. She ducked just in time for the fiery piece of wood to miss hitting her but, as she did, she pushed up against the stall that was already consumed by flames.

Her nightgown caught fire and she could feel her leg burn just before she felt her body being pushed to the ground by a weight too heavy to fight.

She bucked, trying to get back up.

"Stop moving! You're blasted nightgown is on

fire and I'm trying to put it out before you go up in flames like this barn."

Titus had thrown his heavy jacket over her and was hitting at her to extinguish the flames.

"I told you to get out and stay out of here!" The fire must have been out on her nightgown because he reached down and picked her up. When he stood with her in his arms, she gasped in shock to see Wally standing there pawing at the ground. *Why had he come back in?*

"Here Wally, take this fool girl back outside and keep here there!" Titus threw her up onto the mule's back and, as though he understood, Wally raced out of the barn as fast as his body would move him.

When they got outside, she hopped down off Wally's back and bent over to look where her leg had been burned. She still had Titus's heavy jacket covering her, which she was thankful for when she realized how much her nightgown had been damaged.

Her leg had a large red blister, and even as she looked at it, she was sure she could see more blisters forming around it.

Wally put his head down and sniffed at it, then lifted it back up to nudge her to pet him.

"Oh Wally, what are we going to do now? What if Titus can't get the rest of the horses out?" As she stood there watching the barn burn to the ground that Walter had built, she felt tears stream down her cheeks.

Two more of the horses ran out of the barn and she held her breath waiting for Titus and the last one to run out. *Where was he?*

The barn was almost completely gone and she worried knowing his chances to get out the door were running out. She started to move toward the door, just as the entire building collapsed in flames.

CHAPTER 6

H e heard Ella scream his name just as the building started to crumble around him into ashes. He slapped the last remaining horse hard to get her moving and took a step to avoid falling debris as he watched the horse make it out. He was almost at the doorway as the final pieces of wall and roof started to fall in, pinning him beneath a burning piece of wood. He tugged hard on his leg, feeling the heat from the flames reaching out to him.

He looked up for something to pry the wood from his leg, feeling the flames start to burn through his boot. As he lifted his head, he saw the exact moment Ella noticed he was in trouble and start to race toward the burning pile of rubble.

"Stay back there Ella!" He didn't need her coming in any closer in case the last few pieces of wood came down. She wasn't listening to him and kept coming closer until he saw Wally come up behind her and push her aside as he trotted over to him.

"Come here, boy!" Wally was over pushing at the boards with his nose, howling in pain every time he got burned, but he kept pushing them away. When he got close enough, Titus wrapped his arms around the mule's neck. Wally backed away as hard as he could, pulling Titus with him. His boot came off as the mule pulled, tugging him until they were away from the flames.

Titus let go, and collapsed on the ground, pulling his bandana down from his face so he could breathe in the fresh air. His lungs felt like they were on fire and, as he laid there, he realized he had some burns on his hands and arm. His neck felt like it was burning and he reached up, wincing in pain as he realized the burn extended up his neck and to the bottom of his jaw.

He didn't even remember getting burned, he'd been so intent on getting the horses out.

Wally pushed at his shoulders, then moved up and licked at his face.

"Stop it you flea-bitten mule!" He wasn't really mad at Wally, so he said the words softer than he normally did. In fact, he knew, without the mule, he'd likely still be stuck in the burning rubble.

"Titus, are you all right?" Ella landed on the

ground beside him with a thud onto her knees as she peeled back the sides of his shirt that had been scorched beyond repair. He'd just thrown it on for cover as he realized there was a fire and hadn't even managed to get it buttoned up.

Between her and Wally pushing at him, he had to roll onto his side to get away from it. Everywhere they touched burned, so he needed to put some distance between them.

"I'm fine if you two would stop fussing over me. Just let me lay here for a minute to catch my breath."

He went onto his back again and felt bad when he saw the worry in Ella's eyes as she leaned away from him. He could see she'd been crying.

Throwing his arm up onto his forehead, he took a big gulp of air. "Did all of the horses get out?"

He could see her nodding from where he was looking out under his arm. "They did but a couple of them have ran off. I'm not sure we'll catch them again."

The animals in the other pens were snorting and pawing at the ground as the smoke filled the air. Thankfully, when Walter built the barn, he had the forethought to keep it away from anything else in case of a fire and had built a ridge of dirt around the bottom to keep it from spreading quickly. So, everything else would likely be safe but all of the feed and equipment they used for the horses had just been destroyed with the barn.

Not to mention the horses they may not get back.

He let a low groan out and wished he could take it back as soon as Ella leaned in to start fussing over him again.

He lay on the ground, listening to the animals around him and the crackling of the boards still burning. He knew he needed to get up and start hauling water from the creek to get the fire out and make sure it didn't spread further. Even with the separation between the buildings, he knew a spark could set anything else off too.

He sat up and pulled his other boot off. No sense trying to walk with just one boot on.

Standing, he grabbed a couple of buckets sitting beside the animal pens and started to run to the creek. Dipping them in, he filled them and turned, almost running straight into Ella as she raced down with buckets in her hands.

With Wally right on her heels.

The poor animal was likely terrified and afraid to let them out of his sight.

Ella stopped and looked at him with squinted eyes, daring him to say anything. He just shook his head as he raced back to start pouring the water on. He knew there was no sense arguing anyway.

For the next few hours, they ran back and forth,

dumping water on the grounds around the barn to make sure it wasn't going to spread. He wasn't too worried about it getting past the barn but he had to consider sparks that could make it to the other animals and the fences surrounding everything.

He tried to tell her to go in the house and put sensible clothes on, at least, but she had done exactly as expected and completely ignored him.

Wally had calmed down a bit now as he realized he wasn't in any danger and had laid down by the steps to the house.

The sun was coming up over the fields when the last of the burning embers turned to ash. They'd saved everything else but the barn was nothing but a pile of smoldering rubble. When he threw the last bucket of water on the ground, he set the pail down and pushed his hands through his hair. He was covered in soot and dirt, and when he looked over at Ella who was standing and staring at the ruins of the barn, holding her now empty bucket, he saw she was covered too.

Her once white nightgown was almost completely black. At some point, she'd shed the jacket he'd thrown over her. Her hair was hanging limply down all around her face and the color was almost as black as her brother Colton's.

She turned to look at him, and all he could see were the wet trails going down her cheeks from the tears that made their way through the dirt.

He swallowed hard. He'd never been good at offering comfort to anyone but Ella, standing there with her shoulders down in defeat, caused his heart to lurch. Walking over to her, he pulled her into his arms.

"It's going to be all right Ella. We can rebuild this."

She let him hold her and when he felt her arms go around his waist, his heart did something he wasn't familiar with. It had been a long while since a woman had put her arms around him and he couldn't remember it ever being one he actually wanted to offer comfort to.

"I know Titus, but...do you think this was done on purpose?" She said it so quietly he had to strain to hear what she said with her face in his chest.

He didn't want to answer her. She didn't need to be scared. But, he had no doubt it had been done on purpose. He clenched his jaw, peering out at the ground behind her littered with debris.

"I heard something just before the fire started. I thought it was just you but, now, I think maybe it was someone here." She pulled back and looked up at him and he realized she was genuinely afraid. She seemed to understand now that whoever was doing this was prepared to do whatever they had to do to force them all to leave.

"I think maybe you should go back home and stay there. It was foolish to bring you here to try drawing this thief out. We've spread the word that you inherited everything, that's good enough. As far as anyone else knows, I can just be staying on to help out for a bit." He was regretting the decision to bring her here.

The thief had to have heard by now that Ella inherited everything. Now, she could be in danger and he had hardly thought about that. He'd been so intent on bringing the thief out in the open, thinking they'd won, believing it would be easy to get the land from a woman.

But, whoever it was obviously didn't care if it was a man or a woman they were up against. They were going to do whatever they had to do.

She was already shaking her head. "No Titus. I need to be here. This is mine too. And, how would it look for the person who is supposed to have inherited everything to not even live here?" She pulled herself out of his arms and wrapped her arms around herself. She looked at the ground. "They likely figure with this last problem, you'll just leave since you don't need to stay and help a fledgling farm being run by a woman." She looked so small standing in the yard, covered in dirt and ashes, wearing nothing but her tattered nightgown.

He felt his breath catch as she lifted her eyes back to his. "I wouldn't blame you if you left either. There's not much left here to keep fighting for."

"I'm not leaving Ella. I need to find out who

killed my brother, my uncle, and who now just about added me to that list. And, I certainly wouldn't be leaving you here alone to face whoever is doing this." He reached out his hands and gently squeezed her upper arms.

"You go get cleaned up. I'm going to head down to the creek to wash up and then we need to sit down and decide what to do from here. I don't like the thought of you being out here anymore."

She opened her mouth and he was bracing for an argument when he heard the sound of hooves racing into the yard. He turned, hoping to see one of the horses scared off in the fire.

Garett Jackson rode in, leaping from his horse and running toward them. Titus hadn't even realized he was still holding Ella's arms and she was standing in nothing but her nightgown. He dropped his hands quickly but not before seeing the other man's eyes looking back and forth between them.

"I smelled smoke this morning and when I looked over this direction, I could see it in the sky. I came as fast as I could. What happened?" He walked toward the pile of burned wood on the ground, shaking his head. He looked at Titus. "Did you lose much?"

He walked over to stand beside the man. "A couple of horses got spooked and ran off. And, all of the gear in the barn and some feed." He didn't want to let on how bad it really was.

Garett was still shaking his head. "What a shame." He turned and looked at Titus. "But, don't you worry. Your neighbors will all get together and we'll help you rebuild." He slapped Titus hard on the back.

He saw Ella about to make her way to where they were standing but he caught her eye and gave a slight shake of his head, then nudged his head in the direction of the house. She stopped, then looked down, seeming to finally remember she was only wearing a nightgown. And, that nightgown barely had anything left to it. He watched as she turned to head back to the house. He suddenly had the urge to pick her up and carry her when he noticed her limping. He hadn't even noticed she'd been hurt.

When he turned back to face Garett, he saw him watching her too.

He hoped the damage to Ella's reputation hadn't just been destroyed with the barn.

CHAPTER 7

"**E**lla."

The sound of her name broke through
the haze of sleep. She opened her eyes and fought
the confusion. Where was she? Had that all been a
dream?

"Ella, wake up. I've brought you some water
from the creek so you can have yourself a bath and
get cleaned up." Titus's voice cleared the rest of the
fog from her brain. It hadn't been a dream.

Sitting up on the bed, she turned to face him.
He was standing near the tub he'd pulled out for her
to use. She could see steam coming from the water.

"You didn't have to do that for me. I was just
going to rest for a few minutes until Garett left. I
must've fallen asleep." She wondered how long she'd
slept for.

Titus was already cleaned up, wearing some of

Walter's clothes that she'd left hanging in the back. Her heart jumped as she recognized Walter's hat sitting on Titus's head.

"I didn't have anything left after the fire, so had to use a few things of Walter's." He shrugged. "His boots are a bit small but will do until I can get into town to pick up some things. I'm going to head in later today if you want to come." He took the hat off his head and she noticed his hair was still wet from washing in the creek.

She hadn't even thought about all of the things Titus would've had in the barn.

She pulled her blanket up around her, suddenly feeling nervous to have him standing so close to her in just her nightgown. She'd been too tired to even change out of it, sure she'd just rest her eyes for a moment when she'd laid down.

He looked uncomfortable too. "How's your leg?" He lifted his chin to point in her direction.

She could feel it throbbing where the blisters had formed but didn't want him to worry. "It's fine. Just a bit sore." She took in the burns on the side of his neck and jaw and she realized he was trying to keep them hidden by the collar he had done up tightly. She looked down and saw burns on his hands as well.

Suddenly not feeling shy, she threw the cover back and jumped from the bed. It wasn't like he hadn't seen her running around in her nightgown through the whole night and part of the morning anyway.

She pulled down a battered old box she'd found when cleaning up the house, and looked for the bottle of salve she'd seen inside. She turned with a smile on her face and held it up for him to see. He squinted his eyes at her suspiciously. "What's that?"

"Some salve I found when cleaning up. Come sit over here on the chair so I can put some on your burns. You don't want them getting infected."

"I can do it myself."

She huffed some air out and shook her head. "I'm sure you can Titus but can't you just let me do this for you? You just carried buckets of water up for me and warmed them up, so I could have a bath. I would think the least I could do is put some salve on your burns."

He didn't move from the spot he was standing, so she just shrugged and walked toward him. "Fine. I'll just do it standing there."

She took one of his hands and cringed when she saw how bad the burns really were. He was going to need to wrap them up with some gauze or at least some kind of bandage. "Oh Titus, how are you going to be able to work in the fields and do anything with these burns?"

She looked up at him, letting out a small gasp. "It must've hurt to carry the buckets up here with water." She felt guilty, knowing she'd been sleeping while he carried the water for her bath.

He wasn't meeting her eyes, keeping his gaze down on the hand she was holding in front of her. She noticed him swallow.

"Wasn't too bad."

Why did men have to be so stubborn and act tough all the time? She rolled her eyes, then went back to examining the burns. She squeezed some of the lotion on then gently rubbed it in. "I think I have some old cloths in the back you can use to wrap these up. They're clean, I washed them." She grabbed his other hand and did the same, ignoring how fast her heart had started beating being this close to Titus.

She was being a silly girl, letting a man get her all flustered. It was just Titus; it's not like it was a man who'd been courting her and paying her attention.

She didn't lift her head, afraid to meet his eyes. Now she was wishing she'd just let him do it himself. Why didn't she ever think things through more carefully?

They were standing so close, she could smell the soap he'd used, even though the smell of smoke still hung in the air, coming in the windows and from her own body. She could see his chest rising and falling as he breathed but he wasn't saying anything either.

She had to get away from being this close to

him. She, suddenly, felt like she was being burned all over again. Taking a step back, she looked up and met his eyes. They were as dark as night. His jaw was clenched tight, and she could see him swallow again.

"Here, you can finish up on the rest of your burns. Just bring it back in for me to use when you're done." She thrust the tube into his hands and turned, crossing her arms in front of her. She knew she still had to look a mess, so she found her hand going up to try smoothing her soot-filled and matted hair. What must he be thinking of her right now?

And, why did she suddenly care so much?

"I'll be back in a while to carry the water out for you. Then we can figure out what supplies we need to buy and head into town." He cleared his throat. "Maybe we could stay in town for the church dance they are having later today."

She'd forgotten all about that. Every now and then the small community of Bethany would have get-togethers to allow the townsfolk a chance to rest and visit. Tonight they were having a dance outside the church since the nights were so warm.

Titus was actually willing to go to that? She faced him, lifting an eyebrow as she cocked her head to the side. "You want to stay in town for the dance? Are you not feeling well?" A few weeks ago, she'd mentioned that she might go when the family was talking about it and he'd scoffed at her brothers for letting a woman drag them to something like a church dance.

He rolled his eyes. "I'm feeling just fine. I thought it might be a nice way to take your mind off everything. It's been a rough few weeks. Wouldn't hurt for us to have some fun."

She appreciated the thought. Even though he could be a grump, she was finding the more time she spent with him, the more she realized that was just a show he put on for people. She wasn't sure why he bothered but she was learning he was someone who held himself at a distance from people.

She gave him a weak smile, the strength from her body having been sapped from her over the night. "I'd like that very much."

He nodded, then turned to leave. "Get yourself cleaned up though. You look like you've been dragged behind a plow through the mud."

She felt her smile widen. There was the Titus she knew.

❧

BY THE TIME they got cleaned up, took stock of what all they'd lost in the fire, and then drove the wagon to town, there was already a good gathering of townsfolk near the church grounds setting up tables and putting out food.

They quickly picked up the necessary items at the feed store and the mercantile and Titus changed into some clothes he was able to pick up, including some new boots. They drove over to the church just as Colton and Phoebe were pulling up.

"Thought you wouldn't be caught dead at a church dance?" Colton was grinning as he hopped down to go around and help his pregnant wife down from the wagon. Phoebe's younger sister Grace was smiling from the back.

Titus wasn't in the mood for joking around. He was tired, he was angry, and the only reason he was doing this was to try and let Ella have something to smile about.

But he sure as fire wouldn't be telling Colton that.

He didn't even know why he'd offered in the first place. The thought hadn't even entered his mind until he'd seen her bent over head, carefully tending to his burns, while she was still covered in soot and dirt herself. It'd taken every ounce of strength he had to not pull her into his arms.

He had to remember why he kept his distance from women.

He would never let himself be like his father. And, his pa had told him enough times to make him believe that he was already just like him.

So, with his father's words in the back of his mind, he made sure he never let his heart get caught up by a woman.

However, he was afraid to admit to himself, with Ella, it might already be too late.

He needed to keep his focus and remember why he was here. Then, he could be on his way back home, where he could spend his days making sure his father never got his hands on anyone else. He had failed his mother, let her down when she needed someone to stand up for her.

He glanced around at the people starting to gather, figuring whoever was responsible was most likely right under their noses. He was determined he was going to take a more active approach in finding the culprit after last night.

After Colton set Phoebe on the ground, then helped Grace out behind her, he came over to stand by their wagon. Titus hadn't got out yet, still trying to convince himself he could go through with spending a night at a dance.

"We were all going to head over after hearing about the fire but Logan came back after being there and told us you were headed to town for supplies. We were going to make sure we found you." Logan had come along shortly after Ella had gotten cleaned up, having heard about the fire from Garett. He helped them pick through some of the rubble to look at what could be salvaged, if anything, and helped them make the list of what they needed. He'd gone back home then to get cleaned up himself, saying he would let the family know.

Colton looked past Titus toward Ella who was still sitting on her seat too. "So, are you going to come back home now and let Titus deal with this?"

"Colton, I'm tired and I don't want to talk about this right now. I'm here to have some fun and to relax. If you want to start a fight, I assure you, I'm not someone you should be messing with right now." The smile she sent to her brother was the sweetest one Titus had ever seen on her face.

He almost laughed out loud at the look on Colton's face.

"Colton, Ella's right. Leave her alone. She doesn't have to make any decisions right now. Let's all just have some fun, without you trying to butt your nose in where it doesn't belong." Colton's wife, Phoebe, placed her hand on his arm, turning him to face her. She gave him the sweetest smile too and Titus finally did laugh out loud. Poor Colton didn't have a chance.

"Look, I'm in agreement with you that Ella shouldn't be out there anymore but I've also learned that sometimes what is right isn't always so easy to convince her of. So, for now, I just suggest we let the ladies have some fun and we can stand around and pretend we are too." With that, Titus hopped down from his seat and walked over to help Ella down.

He'd already seen more than one person turn their way as they approached, no doubt already talking about him escorting Ella to the dance and the fact that they were living out on Walter's farm together.

Why had he ever thought this would be a good idea? He silently cursed the blonde-haired woman who'd stolen his good sense long enough to ask her to go to a church dance.

CHAPTER 8

"So, do you have any ideas who is responsible? You said you thought you heard something behind the barn that woke you up." Logan was standing beside Titus eating a cookie he had picked off a tray on his way by. The women were all over talking with Susan O'Hara from the mercantile, so the brothers had all closed in on Titus in one sweep, along with James O'Hara and Garett Jackson.

The others all kept their eyes on him and he suddenly wished he was back home with Wally. The news had traveled fast about the barn and he'd been dealing with people coming up to him all evening patting him on the back, assuring him they'd help him rebuild the barn for Ella if he chose to stay and oversee it. Of course, as far as any of them were concerned, he was nothing more than a hired man who'd stayed on to help.

The only ones who knew any different were the Wallaces and James O'Hara who was a close family friend.

He needed to be careful how much he said, making sure Garett didn't figure out the truth. Not that the man was any threat. He was a scrawny man with a mustache that hung almost to his shoulders. He had been friends with Walter for years, even though he was much younger, and had helped him many times on the farm.

Titus suspected he might also have his eye on Ella. He'd noticed him watching her more than once tonight. He wasn't sure why but the thought irritated him more than it should.

Henry Carsen walked up to the group and nodded his head in greeting to the others. He turned to face Reid. "So, since you're the eldest Wallace, are you now gonna try convincing your sister she's on a fool mission to hold on to that farm? I made the offer right after Walter died to buy the farm and the offer still stands. Why on earth would you allow her to stay out there, struggling to save a farm beyond saving, and with a strange man to boot?" Henry wasn't well liked around town and he was known for saying exactly what was on his mind without thinking it through. Now, the man stood shaking his head in disgust that her brothers would allow this to happen.

"B'sides, I don't even reckon it's legal for her to

hold her own property, so one of you likely has legal authority to take it from her if you want as her rightful guardians."

Titus noticed Reid clenching his fists at his sides and he worried the man was about to lose his cool with Henry. Titus didn't like the other man either but he didn't want to cause a scene. Especially since he highly suspected the man was behind everything. He just had no way of proving it. He needed Henry to believe they were all on the same side.

Before he could speak, Logan looked over at Henry. "I assure you that everything Walter put in his will was legal and binding. He went over everything with a fine tooth comb making sure Ella could have the right to own that property."

Logan never mentioned anything about Titus having ownership too.

"Well, whatever the case is, you all need to be thinking about her safety and her ability to manage a farm on her own. I've made no secret of my desire to buy that land and I'm prepared to still buy it, even with all of the problems you all are facing."

Henry had money and he always wanted more, worrying that anyone else would have something more valuable than him. Titus wasn't sure why he wanted Walter's land so badly when he already had his own but there had to be a good reason.

"Now Henry, you know the neighbors are all going to pull through and help Ella rebuild the barn out there. That's what we do in these parts." Garett Jackson spoke up.

Henry smirked and shook his head. "Do you honestly believe that's going to make any difference? There's no way a woman on her own can keep a farm going. No way. Even with a new barn, which I won't be helping build. What's the sense when it will likely be burned to the ground too?"

Titus stepped forward. "Is that a threat Henry?" His voice was low but he made sure there was no doubt of Henry hearing him. "Because I'll tell you right now, Ella won't be on her own out there. And, I will make sure I catch whoever is trying to run her off."

He knew he was treading on dangerous ground and should be letting the others think he didn't care one way or another. But, the man was getting under his skin and he didn't want Henry to think he could get to Ella.

Henry just laughed and shook his head while looking at each of the men in turn. "You're all fools if you can't even see what's going on. And, now that she's ruined her reputation by staying out there with a man we all know isn't her husband, you can forget about any other man stepping in to take over responsibility of her and that farm."

He looked at Reid. Titus had to step in front of Ella's brother when he noticed the clenched jaw and redness on the other man's face as he moved to step toward Henry.

"If you're prepared to leave your sister out there to keep pretending she has a chance of keeping that farm, then I question your sanity." Henry obviously didn't realize the dangerous position he was in. Every one of Ella's brothers were standing with fists clenched and muscles twitching. Titus didn't think he could hold them all back.

"Just ignore him. He'll get what's coming to him." Titus spoke but he didn't know if any of the brothers heard him as they all kept their eyes glued to Henry's face.

Henry just laughed as he turned and walked away.

"Doesn't that man realize how easy it is to figure out he's the one behind all of the thefts and most likely even the barn fire? He sure isn't tryin' very hard to hide it." Garett was shaking his head as he watched the man walk away.

"Well, he's lucky he even has two legs to walk away on right now." Reid spoke through clenched teeth.

"What did Henry want?" Ella's voice startled Titus. He hadn't even heard her come up.

"Just trying to find out if you'd be willing to sell to him now. We let him know you wouldn't be interested." He watched as she squinted her eyes at the back of the man who was now talking to another group next to the church steps. He almost laughed at the expression that mimicked all of the brothers who were standing around them.

"Well, he's not getting it that easy. If he thinks burning the barn to the ground will make me give up, then he obviously doesn't know me at all." She lifted her chin slightly and Titus had to smile. He gave his head a shake.

"No, I told him as much." Titus was happy to see she had a bit of spark in her still. He'd been worried, seeing her look so beaten this morning after the fire.

The musicians started to play, signaling the time for dancing. "Ella, would you like to dance?" Garett reached his arm out for her to take. He looked over at Titus. "If'n it's all right with you?" Titus ground his teeth together.

"Don't matter to me one way or the other." He would never let on to anyone around him how much he really didn't like it one bit. But, it wasn't really his place to say otherwise.

The men stood and watched Garett lead Ella out to the area between the tables that were lit up with lanterns now as the sun went down.

By now, Audrey and Phoebe had both walked over, putting their hands out for their husbands to take them out for a dance, leaving only Titus and Logan standing there. Grace was off talking with some other young girls from the area.

"For someone who doesn't care one way or another, you sure can't seem to find anything else to glare at." Logan had reached out and grabbed another cookie, popping the entire thing in his mouth at once.

Titus was able to find someone else to move his stare to and Logan just laughed when he noticed it was now aimed at him.

❧

THE SOUNDS of the fiddle lifted her spirits and the problems of the barn and everything else back at the farm were forgotten for a short time. She was glad Titus had agreed to come to the dance, although she likely would've come with one of her brothers anyway.

As Logan spun her around, she laughed and ignored the sour look on Titus's face from where he stood by one of the tables of food. She could see he wasn't enjoying himself and she knew she should feel bad that he came just for her. But he wasn't even trying to have fun, so she couldn't feel too sorry for him.

The tables were set up in a square, leaving room in the middle for some bales of hay that had been pulled in to sit on. Each table was filled with food and drink brought by the women and, all around the area, lanterns lit up the sky.

Children raced around playing while the adults talked and danced. Bethany was a small community and the townsfolk and people in the area all worked hard to settle the land they had chosen for their homes. So, they tried to have as many get-togethers as possible to let them relax and renew their hope for their future in Oregon.

Ella wouldn't ever want to live anywhere else. The people around her were like family and she smiled as she recognized so many people she knew.

There'd been a few new settlers to the area and one of the families had a daughter around her age she'd hoped to become friends with at one time. But, from what she'd seen at church, and now tonight, she didn't think they would become friends any time soon. Connie McGinley was a spoiled, pampered girl who did nothing but whine and complain.

As Logan threw her out for another spin, she caught Connie walking toward Titus. Ella almost tripped over her own feet as she tilted her head to make sure she could see what was going on.

"Ella, if you're so worried about what Connie is saying to Titus, why don't you go ask him to dance yourself?" Logan was grinning at her as he grabbed her arm and whipped her around.

"I don't care Logan and why don't you mind your own business." Logan just gave a low chuckle in his throat and pulled her around in a circle.

"You're as stubborn as he is."

She tried to get him to slow down sure, by now, her hair would be hanging in a mess all around her at the amount of spinning Logan was doing.

"Maybe it's you who's jealous and don't like Connie talking to another man." She laughed at the sudden change of expression on Logan's face. He'd been getting endless teasing about the new girl in town since he was one of the most eligible bachelors left in the area. She also knew exactly what Logan thought about the girl who'd whined endlessly in church one day about the hard benches they sat on.

The song ended, thankfully, before Ella had been spun right out of her shoes. Logan laughed as he led her back over to the table by Titus. Everyone else had found a place to sit or were up dancing, so Titus was left standing with no choice but to speak to Connie when she'd gone over to him.

As they approached, Ella couldn't help but compare herself to the other woman. Even though she was independent and believed she was as strong as many men, Ella still felt the insecurities of a woman.

Connie had long, thick, wavy black hair that hung perfectly from beneath the satin bonnet she wore on her head. Her stunning emerald green dress fit snugly, showing her tiny waist and, as she talked to Titus, she smiled coyly at him, batting lashes that outlined eyes that perfectly matched the color of her dress.

Ella quickly looked down and realized she was wearing one of her Sunday best dresses but it had small tears on the edges from wear. It was a flowery material, made out of sturdy fabric. It definitely wasn't something that would catch a man's eye.

She reached up to try smoothing her hair a bit, knowing it would be a mess after the dancing. As she did, she looked over and caught Titus watching her. He gave her a quick smile, not paying attention to what Connie was saying.

"Titus, aren't you going to ask me to dance?" The woman tapped him on his arm with the fan she was still carrying around, even though it wasn't as hot as it had been earlier in the day.

"Well, I would, but I promised Ella the next dance." Ella almost fell over as he grabbed her by the arm and practically dragged her back out to the area designated for dancing.

"Titus, stop manhandling me like I'm a sack of feed for the horses!" She was sure her arm had been stretched an inch from the pulling.

"Sorry, but I had to get away from that blasted woman and you were the best chance I had." He turned around and took her in his arms, grinning down at her with amusement in his eyes.

"You really know how to sweet talk a girl, don't you? There is nothing a woman loves more than to know the reason you're dancing with her is to get away from someone else." She was annoyed and she wasn't sure if it was from the actual comment he'd made or the sudden pounding in her chest.

Why did he seem to have this effect on her?

As he started moving around with her, so much gentler and slower than her brother had done, she could almost imagine how it must feel to have someone put their arms around you for real.

But, she knew this wasn't for real. This was a man who was performing a job until he could leave and go back home. And, he was dancing with her for no other reason than to escape an option he felt was worse.

Her heart dropped to her stomach as she looked up and met his eyes. Suddenly, she realized the feelings she was starting to have for him were real in her heart. But, there was nothing she could do about it.

CHAPTER 9

The sound of pounding hammers made her
smile. She knew Walter would be smiling
down too. Everywhere she looked, there were
people hauling lumber, hammering, cutting and
lifting boards. The men from the area had already
arrived, tools in hand and ready to help them
rebuild the barn.

The morning had been spent hauling away the
burned boards and ashes from the site where the
barn had once stood. Now, as she watched, there
was already a frame for what would soon be her new
barn.

She was sure everyone from town was here
except, of course, for Henry Carson. He had been
adamant he wouldn't help on a fool's mission.

What she couldn't understand was, if he wanted
this property so badly, wouldn't he want a nice new

barn standing on it? Not that she'd ever let him get his hands on it anyway.

"I should be out there helping them. They all think they're here building this barn just for me and it doesn't seem right that I'm not out there sweating with the rest of them." Ella placed a pitcher of lemonade on the table they had moved outside. Thankfully, when Phoebe, Grace and Audrey had arrived, they brought some utensils and necessary items to host a meal for the entire community. Walter hadn't had much more than a few tin plates, a pot to cook in, some cups and a bit of cutlery.

"Ella, they need to be fed and made sure to have cool drinks ready for them. They all know what they're doing. This isn't the first time they've worked together to build something for a family in the area." Audrey placed some fresh biscuits on the table, while Ella's mother Anna set out a couple pies.

They'd built a fire outside and Titus had brought out the hanging bar from inside to make the stew over the fire. They had two pots hanging, the air around them filled with the aroma of the food cooking. Wally had to be tied up next to the house, having wandered too close to the men who were working and taking their tools.

When he'd been brought up here, he'd almost knocked the table over with the food. He wasn't happy now and was snorting loudly to express his displeasure.

The men all started walking toward the fire, throwing their tools down now that the smell of the food was reaching them. Her heart swelled with happiness as she watched all of these men who had come out to help. Some of them she didn't know well at all but they were here anyway, helping out a fellow community member who needed a hand.

And, it wasn't just men. Susan O'Hara from the mercantile had closed for the day to come out with her husband and was helping with the cooking and Dorothy Larsen from the boardinghouse was standing over one of the pots dishing out the stew into bowls.

Ella couldn't keep the smile off her face as she cut the pies in front of her into pieces, then lifted them on to plates for the men.

"Nice to see you smilin' Ella." Garett was moving through the line and took a piece of apple pie from her hands.

"Well, it's just heartwarming to see the people all come and help. I've seen it done a hundred times since I've lived here but it's never been for me. I guess I didn't appreciate how much it would mean." She gave the man a friendly smile before turning to lift a piece of pie for the next man in line.

She dished up the food and busied herself going around and pouring drinks for everyone. She took the opportunity to thank everyone and let them know how much she appreciated it. When she got to the tree where Titus was sitting with her family, she felt her stomach somersault. Seeing him sitting with everyone else like he was already a member of the family shocked her. She suddenly realized how nice it would be to have a husband who truly belonged there, with her.

Instead, it was Titus and even if she was starting to have feelings for him she couldn't quite explain, she knew he didn't feel the same way.

"Ella dear, you better sit down and have a bite to eat too. You haven't stopped moving since this morning, and you look about ready to collapse." She suddenly realized she was hungry when her mother reminded her, so she grabbed herself a bowl of stew and sat down on the blanket beside Audrey.

She noticed Titus lift his eyebrows at the obvious refusal to sit on the full extra side of blanket he was on, instead of forcing Audrey and Reid to share theirs.

No one spoke for a while which she found strange for her family. She lifted her eyes as she brought her spoon to her mouth and caught everyone casting nervous glances at each other.

She could feel her eyebrows wrinkle together. "What's going on? Why are you all looking at each other like that?" She noticed her brothers all look over at Titus who was now avoiding looking at her. He kept his eyes on the barn behind her.

She turned and looked at Phoebe. Out of everyone, she knew her sister-in-law wouldn't be afraid to tell her the truth.

"Ella, it's nothing. It's just these brutes of brothers of yours who think there's a problem." Phoebe shook her head. "Some people seem to forget that things aren't always what they seem and they shouldn't let other people believe the worst." The last sentence was directed at Colton.

Ella set her bowl down, no longer hungry. "What are you talking about?"

"There's been some talk today around the barns. We've all heard it, even though I know most of the people are trying to keep it from reaching our ears." Colton replied, keeping his eyes from his wife's.

"What kind of talk?" She asked, even though she knew already what it would be.

"The kind of talk people need to learn to keep to themselves." Audrey reached over and patted her on the arm. "Don't worry Ella. Most of the townsfolk around here know you and they know our family. They aren't going to believe the worst."

Ella's heart sunk. Where she'd been feeling so happy just moments ago and so full from the support of the people around her, she now realized that some of them also had their doubts about whether she should be living out here on her own with a hired man.

She looked over and met Titus's eyes. He was watching her, not saying a word.

"There's been some talk questioning why Titus would stay here now that Walter's gone and it's just you left here to pay him. And, now that the barn is gone, some of the people have been asking questions about where he's been sleeping." Logan filled her in on the rest.

She closed her eyes and reached up to pinch the bridge of her nose where she could suddenly feel a headache.

"I told you all that he's sleeping outside. He made a tent out of the canvas left from Walter's wagon and has tied it to the back of the lean-to." She didn't even open her eyes as she spoke. "Everyone could see it if they turned their heads to look."

"Oh Ella dear, we don't have any doubts or questions about anything but you know how people talk. It's not us you have to convince." Her mother's voice helped her to open her eyes.

"We think it'd be best if you come home and stay there until Titus leaves for home." Reid's voice left no room for argument.

However, she was in the mood to give him one anyway.

"I don't care what anyone thinks is best. I'm

staying here, with my farm, and if people want to go around saying things about my reputation, then they aren't the kind of people I want to know anyway."

"Ella, be reasonable. You know this will hurt any chance you'll have of getting married. Most men won't want to marry someone they believe would sully their good name to stay on a farm with a man who isn't their husband. If there were others around or if Titus was older and not likely to be attracted to you, maybe it wouldn't be so hard to believe but after seeing the two of you dancing the other night, some of the people from town have their suspicions." She turned and glared at Colton, daring him to say anything more.

"I danced with many men that night, why are they only fussing about me and Titus dancing?" She knew why but she was itching for a fight, and couldn't seem to stop herself.

"Because I'm sleeping out here on the farm with you, with no one else around to make sure we aren't doing anything that wouldn't be considered 'proper' by the fine people of this community." Titus answered for her.

"Titus, that's not fair. It isn't everyone in the community. In fact, most of the people I've spoken to know Ella wouldn't do anything like that. It's mostly some of the newer settlers to the area who are trying to stir up some gossip." James O'Hara,

Susan's husband, explained. "In fact, it was Douglas McGinley who I overheard mentioning it."

Douglas was Connie's doting father. The apple hadn't fallen far from that tree.

"Of course, I set him straight but he'd already said enough out loud to cause some suspicions."

She stood up, lifting her bowl of untouched stew to give to Wally. "I know what people are saying and I know what they're thinking. But, I already told you. I'm not going home. This is all I have that's mine. It's all I'll ever have that'll be mine." She could feel tears starting to form and she was shaking from embarrassment, wishing she could hold her emotions together long enough to say what she wanted to say.

"I'll never have a husband to love me or children on my knee that are my own." She swallowed hard to push the sob down that was threatening to escape. "Walter left this for me. I may have to share it with Titus but that doesn't mean anything else is going on. If I walk away and let Titus fight for this farm on his own, I'm not only letting Walter down, I'm letting go of the chance to fight for something that's mine."

She started to walk away. She needed to get in the house to pull herself together. Everyone would be leaving soon for the evening but she knew she would need to face them all as she cleaned up and said the goodbyes. And, they'd all be back in the morning.

She knew it wasn't all of the townsfolk who were judging her. In fact, she knew most of the people here would defend her honor if anyone suggested otherwise.

But, there were enough newcomers that were causing a stir and it stung to know they were all talking about her like that. Even though she'd known this would likely happen, she'd secretly hoped they could catch the thief before then and Titus would have moved on.

At the time, she wanted him gone as soon as possible so she could take over the farm for herself. And now that people were talking and she should be wishing the thief was caught so he could go, she was finding herself wishing instead that he would never leave.

CHAPTER 10

The wind picked up, swirling around him. He tried to get comfortable, tossing and turning on the hard ground. He was no stranger to sleeping outside but, tonight, he felt agitated and unable to drift off. The lantern he could see in the window of the small shack across the yard didn't help.

He knew Ella would still be awake and he also knew she was upset. She'd barely spoken for the rest of the evening, cleaning up the food from the day and getting things ready for everyone to come back tomorrow.

Her brothers had helped him finish up the evening chores after everyone else left, while the women helped Ella. He didn't want to admit how much he actually missed having her out there help-ing, arguing with him and talking non-stop about anything she thought he might be interested in knowing about.

And, he could feel the tension with her brothers towards him. He understood they were protective of her but he wasn't sure how they couldn't see by now that she was a determined woman and when she set her mind, nothing would change it.

They'd known her all their lives. He'd only known her a few months and already knew that about her.

But, he also knew that even though she said she didn't care and her reputation didn't matter because she thought she was already past the age of finding someone to love her, everything that people were saying about her now did bother her.

She might say otherwise but he knew she was still holding on to the hope that there'd be a man who would sweep her off her feet and fall in love with her.

Titus groaned to himself and flung his arm over his eyes. He hated the fact that whenever he thought about Ella falling in love and marrying another man, it made his chest feel like it was being squeezed in a grip he couldn't fight.

He knew he had feelings for Ella that'd gone past the point of just being business partners.

But, he also knew there wasn't anything he could do about it. Ella deserved someone who'd treat her like a queen and Titus knew that wouldn't be him. If he ended up even a bit like his father, he knew Ella would end up being hurt and hating him before too long.

That's why he needed to get away from here.

The night sky suddenly lit up, followed by a crack of thunder that shook the ground he was laying on. He sat up and put his boots on, knowing he was going to have to try getting the animals settled. A storm like this could come on fast and it could cause a lot of damage.

They really didn't need this on top of everything else that'd happened.

Wally was over by him immediately. The mule slept out with him beside his makeshift tent and never wandered off so he was never tied up. Now, the mule pushed his nose into Titus's face as he put his other boot on.

"Wally, there's nothing to be scared of. Now, get out of my way." He didn't have the time to coddle the terrified mule. Wally was right behind him as he started to walk over to the horse pens, checking to make sure the gates were latched securely.

All of the animals were pacing and pawing at the ground. He wished he could get them all in somewhere dry and out of the weather but the barn wasn't finished. They'd made good progress today but there was still quite a ways to go.

He just hoped none of them would get spooked too badly and hurt themselves trying to get away.

Before he could finish checking all of the gates, another flash of lightning filled the sky and the thunder came right behind it, cracking so loud it hurt his ears. Immediately, the skies opened and the rain fell so hard it hurt his face.

Wally almost knocked him over running right to his side.

He moved faster now, making sure everything was taken care of. He glanced up to the house and caught a glimpse of a shadow standing in the window.

He hadn't even thought about Ella. He hoped the storm wouldn't scare her but he knew he should go and check on her.

"Come on Wally, we better go check on Ella." The mule was tucked up as close as he could get, and Titus was sure he'd have fleas on himself by morning for sure.

Before he even got to the top step, Ella whipped the door open. Wally took that as an invitation and ran through the door before either of them could stop him. For an animal that had likely faced much hardship in its life, it sure didn't seem to handle scary situations well.

"Just thought I'd come and check to make sure you were all right and all locked down for the night. The storm looks pretty bad." Water poured from the peak of his hat as he stood in the rain outside the door.

"You should come in until the storm passes Titus. You can't be out in this." Her voice sounded nervous and he could see that her face was ashen. She jumped and her hand flew up to her chest as another crack of thunder shook the house. He could see her hand was shaking.

He knew she was scared but didn't want to admit it to him.

"I could come in and sit a while." He could at least get dried off a bit before he had to crawl into his wet blankets.

She nodded, and he could see her chin trembling. "I can make us some tea to warm you up." She went to the fire and busied herself hanging the pot to boil.

Wally was over by her side right away. "Sorry, he followed me here and wouldn't leave my side. Not sure how we can get him back out so long as the storm is raging out there. I've never seen a more sorry excuse for an outdoor animal than that thing." He pulled his wet hat from his head and brought it over to hang by the hook near the fire hoping to dry it.

She just turned and reached out to pat Wally on the neck. "It's fine. He should be in here with us where it's safe anyway."

Titus could only shake his head. What did Ella see in that animal? He'd admit he was grateful that Wally had been there to help him get out of the fire but, for the most part, the mule did nothing to help around the farm.

He went and sat in Walter's chair by the fire. He was soaked through his clothes, so he hoped the heat from the fire would dry him.

Ella kept glancing nervously at him from the corner of her eyes as she pulled out the cups and busied herself around the small kitchen. Whenever she heard another explosion of thunder, her body would tense.

"There might still be a couple of Walter's shirts in the chest near the back if you'd like to change into something dry." She moved over to the chest she was talking about and looked inside. She pulled out a plaid flannel shirt she found, walking over to offer it to him.

He stifled a grin as he noticed her eyes widen when he reached up to start undoing the first button on his shirt, then turn so fast she almost fell over top of Wally trying to get away from him.

He'd flung his shirt off to the side and had the new one just shrugged on when a flash of lightning filled the house with light at the same time the thunder crashed around them. Titus lifted his head and jumped out of his seat at the sound of glass shattering on the ground.

A tree had fallen through a window and now the wind was whipping through the small room, bringing gusts of rain inside with it. He heard Ella scream as he ran over to try covering the opening.

"Grab a blanket or something I can tack up here!" He hollered above the sound of the wind.

Wally was bellowing at the top of his lungs, making the sound inside the room deafening. Ella stood rooted to the spot and he noticed the broken glass at her feet where she must have been holding the cup she'd poured for their tea.

He cursed, then ran over to the chest and grabbed Walter's old, tattered quilt he'd seen in there when she'd opened it before. He knew where the hammer and nails had been when Walter lived here and he was glad to see Ella hadn't moved them during her cleaning.

When he got the quilt covering the window, he stood back and caught his breath. The wind was still whistling between the broken glass and the temporary barrier but at least the rain was staying out. He turned to see Ella still standing in the same spot.

Her eyes were wet from tears and when he walked toward her, he saw her chin trembling as she tried to calm her fears.

"It's fine Ella. The storm'll be over in no time." He saw her swallow as she met his eyes. They were wide and a brighter blue than he'd ever seen them and, as he got closer, he noticed she was blinking quickly trying to stop her tears.

Pulling her into his arms before he realized what

he was doing, he reached up and brought his hand onto the back of her head.

She put her arms around him and held tight. He had to take a deep breath to keep himself under control. Feeling her in his arms like this was causing him to feel emotions he knew were dangerous.

"I'm sorry, Titus. I hate storms. Ever since I was a little girl. I guess this is the first time I've had to be on my own during one, so I got spooked." She spoke into his chest as he rested his chin on the top of her head.

"Well, you're not entirely alone Ella. You have me here and Wally." The animal in question was over nudging them with his nose.

Ella pulled back and looked up at him with a smile. "I know. Thank you Titus."

Before he could stop himself, his head was lowering and he caught her lips beneath his. He hadn't planned to do it but seeing her looking at him like that had broken down any last bit of resistance he had toward her.

He kissed her gently, at first, until he felt her arms pull him closer and he was lost. His lips pushed at hers, as both hands came up to loop through her long hair. Just when he was afraid he was past the point of reason, Wally pushed between them.

They both pulled away, staring at each other without moving. He saw her shoulders rising and falling with each breath. She carefully lifted her fingers to her lips.

"I'm so sorry Ella. I shouldn't have done that." He didn't know what to say. He'd taken advantage of her in her fear.

She still wasn't moving and her eyes were locked on his.

He turned to grab his hat from the hook but he felt her hand reach out for his arm.

"No Titus, please stay. I don't want to be here by myself." Her voice was quiet and it shook when she spoke.

He couldn't turn around. He knew if he looked at her, there would be no going back. Instead, he moved over to the chair. "I'll just stay here until the storm lets up. You get into bed."

He knew he sounded angry and his voice sounded shaky to his own ears.

She never replied but he could hear her feet shuffling across the floor, then the creaking of the mattress as she laid down. He put his feet up on the stool in front of the chair and crossed his arms in front of him.

His lips were still burning from the heat of the kiss and, no matter how hard he tried, he couldn't seem to get his heart back under control. He dimmed the lantern so he couldn't see her laying on the bed.

Just when he thought the storm had finally

passed them by, another crack of thunder, louder than any before, exploded at the exact moment the lightning filled the room. His eyes looked over to Ella just as it struck and he could see her sitting on the bed with her eyes full of tears.

He couldn't let her lay there alone feeling scared no matter how hard it would be for him.

He stood and silently walked over to the bed. "Move over. I will just sit here until the storm passes." He sat down on the edge of the bed and she didn't put up any argument. He knew then how scared she must really be when she wasn't resisting.

She curled up on the other side as far as she could get from him. He leaned his head back and rested it on the pillow behind him, half sitting and half laying. The sound of her even breathing soothed his own, and as he laid there, he heard Wally lay down on the floor by the fire. The crackling of the fire and the sound of the steady rain caused his eyelids to get heavy.

The sound of a door crashing and voices yelling reached to him through a haze.

Where was he? He opened his eyes and saw that somehow, at some time through the night, he'd fallen asleep and he now had his arm around a still sleeping Ella.

"Titus Cain! Do you want to tell me what you are doing in my sister's bed?"

CHAPTER 11

Ella could hear voices yelling but she snuggled back down into her blankets. She felt so warm, so safe. She knew she was dreaming and in her dream, Titus was holding her in her arms. *Why were people yelling?*

Suddenly, she felt the bed move and she realized she hadn't been dreaming. And, the voices she could hear were getting louder.

"You better start explaining Titus or I'll be dragging you outside to answer to me." She could hear Colton's voice over the top of everyone's. She sat up quickly, realizing she needed to figure out what was going on.

"Colton! What are you doing? What's going on?" She needed to clear her head but the exhaustion from yesterday, then the late storm keeping her awake, had caused her to drift into a deep sleep, and she was still in the confused state between sleeping and waking.

As her eyes focused, she could see Phoebe and her mother standing behind Colton and with all of the yelling now, she could see some of the men from town standing outside the open doorway looking in. Everyone had started to arrive to work on the barn but she and Titus had overslept!

And as she looked to him standing beside the bed shoving his hands through his hair, she remembered where he'd fallen asleep last night.

Her stomach sunk right to her feet as she realized what it looked like. Titus looked over at her with a pained expression and she knew what everyone was thinking.

Her reputation was officially ruined. And, her family wasn't happy that the entire town was witness to it.

She swallowed hard. All because she was scared of a storm. The one time she needed to be strong but she couldn't be and now Titus was going to have to face the consequences when he'd only been trying to help her.

What could she even say to anyone to make this right? No one was going to listen. She noticed Phoebe walk over and close the door, so at least the others wouldn't have to see her humiliation.

Her sister-in-law then turned and reached her

hand out to place on Colton's arm. Colton never moved a muscle, focusing his glare on Titus.

"Colton, calm down. You aren't helping anything by acting like a bull on a rampage." Phoebe looked over at her and gave her a sad smile. "I'm sure there's an explanation."

"Oh, I have no doubt there's an explanation and that's exactly why I didn't want my sister living out here with the likes of him!"

"Colton! That's enough. We will hear what Ella has to say." Anna scolded her son then turned to Ella. "Ella, you better have a good explanation for what we've walked into this morning. The fact that Garett Jackson and James O'Hara happened to be here to witness it too isn't going to help your situation. We are just fortunate that both men are family friends. However, there are other people outside this door from town and I have no doubt by now they've figured out what's going on."

Ella could hear her heart beating. She looked around at everyone standing in the room. The only one giving her any hint of a smile was Phoebe. Everyone was angry and she couldn't blame them. Wally had got up during the commotion and was over pushing against her.

Turning to Titus, she realized he hadn't moved from his spot. He knew he'd compromised her and she had no doubt over the guilt he was feeling. It was all over his face.

She swung her legs off the edge of the bed and stood up directly in front of Colton. She could handle her brother; she'd been doing it all her life. "Colton Wallace, you listen to me. You didn't walk in on anything more than two people, completely exhausted from fighting against everything that seems to be working against them, finally getting some much needed sleep. All you saw was a man who'd come in from the storm to keep me from being scared, knowing full well he could get in trouble for it." She could feel her anger rising. The past few weeks of dealing with the loss of Walter, then the fire, while trying to find out who was behind all of it had taken every bit of strength she had in her. And now, because of last night, she might lose it all.

She moved even closer to Colton, raising her hand and pointing her finger to his chest. "And if you hadn't come in here all fired up and yelling loud enough to wake snakes, no one else would be any the wiser. Thanks to you..." She pushed him hard with her finger. "Now everyone outside that door thinks something happened in here that didn't."

Her brother squinted his eyes at her, then lifted to look at Titus. He shook his head, then turned and pushed his hand through his hair, almost knocking his hat off.

"Well, now what are we going to do?"

"We aren't going to do anything. I'm going out

there, setting out the tables and we're all going to act like nothing happened...because it didn't." She turned to face Titus. "I'm sorry you had to get dragged into this and all because my brother is a fool who shouts first and listens later."

Titus looked up to the ceiling and she could see him swallow before he looked back down and met her eyes.

"Ella, it doesn't matter what your brother did. The fact is, people are going to be thinking the worst no matter what. Not many people will be interested in hearing the truth."

She could feel herself shaking and she wasn't sure if it was from anger or fear of what would happen when she walked outside. But, she needed a moment to get herself together.

He pushed himself away from the wall and did up the shirt that he'd never had the chance to fasten the night before. He grabbed his hat and met Colton's glare. "You're free to think what you want but I'd hope by now you'd know the kind of man I am." Then he turned to face Ella.

"I'll go out and try to smooth things over before you have to come out." She felt terrible knowing he was throwing himself outside to face everyone's disapproval, knowing they likely wouldn't give him any chance to explain.

Colton followed him to the door. "I'll go with you." She knew her brother may have a temper and not always think things through before losing it but she knew he'd have Titus's back while facing the others.

"Come on Ella, let's get you ready then start getting the lunch ready for the men." Phoebe came over and took her arm, offering her a smile and a squeeze on her arm as Ella watched Titus and Colton go outside with Wally right on their heels.

Thanks to her, Titus was going outside to defend her reputation to those who'd most likely already made up their minds. She knew there were some who knew her better and who knew she wouldn't have done anything.

But, those weren't the ones she worried about. It was the rest of the people who she knew would likely cause even more problems for her and Titus to face.

She wasn't sure how much more they could take.

❧

TITUS SWUNG THE HAMMER, hitting it against the nail with all his strength. He needed to release his anger and frustration, so working on the barn was helping him work through some of the fury he was feeling.

He wasn't just mad at the few people who were whispering and who'd shook their heads in disapproval as he tried to explain what'd happened.

He was also angry at himself for putting Ella in this position in the first place.

It wasn't his reputation that was ruined. He was a man and, in the eyes of everyone else, what a man did was a man's business. However, for women, it was a different story. And he knew that no matter how much she said it didn't matter and that she didn't care, he knew this was going to affect Ella far more than she even realized.

Bethany was a small community and the people around the area were mostly good, kind-hearted folk who'd struggled to make a life out here in Oregon. But, there were a few who seemed to take delight in other people's downfall.

Unfortunately, one of those people was Douglas McGinley and he was one of the loudest ones this morning saying it wasn't right.

He'd been shouting louder than anyone, saying he didn't know if he wanted to be involved in helping raise a barn for a woman who obviously had questionable morals.

Wally had gone over to Douglas and Titus was almost sure he'd growled at the man if it was even possible.

But, Titus had soon figured out why. Douglas had eyed Wally up, then announced that this was his mule. Obviously, he expected that Wally should be going back to him since it was his property.

Titus had wasted no time letting the other folks

know what bad shape the animal had been left to die in and the only reason it was alive was due to Ella's care. Titus had offered to pay the man for him if he was still going to argue but he had made it clear he'd never allow Wally to be sent back to live in the conditions he'd been found in.

And, the way Wally was snorting at Douglas, it was clear he had no intentions of going back either.

The man had left shortly after but not without making sure everyone knew he believed more had happened with Ella and Titus than they had let on and that they were all fools for helping them. Thankfully, none of the other men had left with him.

But, the damage had been done.

How could he have let himself sleep so deeply? Normally, he was a light sleeper, hearing everything and waking up before the sun rose.

But, he guessed the exhaustion from yesterday, along with being next to a woman who he couldn't quite figure out, had messed with him and he'd slept like the dead. He hadn't even heard anything until Colton came barreling in the door.

He banged his thumb, cursing under his breath as he brought it to his mouth to try and ease the throbbing.

He caught Reid's eye as the other man worked across from him. He knew he wasn't liked much by Ella's brothers at the moment but at least they'd stood behind him. He was sure they believed that nothing had happened. They just weren't particularly happy that their sister was in this situation now.

He should've just stayed in his chair last night. She would've been fine knowing he was in the house at least.

But no, he'd seen the opportunity to get closer to her and, even though he knew it was wrong, he'd done it anyway.

They'd been working all morning and he knew they were going to have to head to the house to eat soon. He'd seen Ella coming in and out a few times, carrying food and setting things out for the men to come and eat. She'd held her head high and not even bothered to pay any attention to the men over working on the barn.

It seemed strange to see her still in her regular dresses this late in the day. Normally, when it was just them working out on the farm, she'd have changed into her split skirts to work with the horses. But she must have figured since she wasn't doing any work with the animals today, she'd just stay in her normal clothes.

His breath caught as he watched her by the table. Her eyes finally scanned the group working on the barn until they found his. He saw her give him a sad smile before turning to go back into the house. He wished he could take that sadness away from her.

Anna walked over to let them know their lunch was ready and he could hear the men all drop their tools to head up to the house. He hesitated, knowing how much everyone was going to be watching them now. He thought maybe he should just keep working.

"Come on Titus, may as well get this over with. We aren't going to let anyone say anything about you or Ella, so don't worry." Logan came over and slapped him on the back as he walked by.

One thing Titus was learning since arriving in Bethany was that the Wallace family stuck together, no matter what. He wished he had a family like that.

He tried to keep his eyes down, afraid of letting anyone see anything between him and Ella. But, he also needed to see for himself that she was all right, so when he got to the place where she was pouring them all some lemonade, he let his eyes find hers.

Hers were shiny from what looked like unshed tears, and he realized that as the men had gone through ahead of them, most of them hadn't been able to look at her as they took their drinks. Even though most of them didn't believe it, they also weren't sure how to act around her now.

The damage had been worse than he'd imagined.

They were all sitting on their spots under the

trees where they ate yesterday, no one saying much, when Garett walked over to the family and sat down on a stump near the edge.

"I um...I know things have got into a bit of a fuddle around here today and I um...well, I just wanted to offer my hand to marry Ella and make sure there is no lasting damage to her reputation." The man had quickly turned to Titus with his cheeks a bright red color. "I know nothing happened with the two of you and I wouldn't step in except for the fact that you've made it clear you have no intentions of staying here. I'd hate to see Ella left here to deal with this all on her own."

Titus ground his teeth as he listened to the other man try to speak his piece. He almost laughed when he saw the confused look on Colton's face as he tried to figure out what to say.

He could see Ella sitting on the other side of her brother, and her face had just gone as white as the first snow of winter.

"Well, that's mighty kind of you to offer, Garett. You've been a good friend of the family and to Walter when he was living. But, that's a decision we have to let Ella make on her own." Reid looked uncomfortable, most likely sure he knew exactly what Ella was going to say.

Garett turned to Ella. "I know I've asked you before and you said you weren't sure we'd be suited. But, this time, I think we all know that if you don't let someone marry you, you'll never be able to repair the damage that was done here today. I'm a good member of the community and I can offer you anything you need. I can give you a home and, maybe someday, we could even have a family..."

Titus couldn't listen to any more. Every time he looked at Ella, he could see the fear and the pain in her eyes, knowing that what Garett was saying was true. Her reputation couldn't be fixed now. And, if she didn't get married, she'd spend the rest of her days being whispered about and shunned. Her eyes met his and he felt his heart stop beating.

"Garett, we appreciate your thoughts for Ella's reputation. However, since I'm the one who did the damage, I'm the one who'll fix it. Ella will be marrying me."

CHAPTER 12

It wasn't how she'd always dreamed her wedding day would be but the past few days had completely ripped away any hope of that happening anyway.

She was angry. And, even though the brunt of her anger was aimed at Titus, her brothers, and the community of Bethany for forcing this marriage, she had to admit that she was angry with herself too. She should never have let this happen.

But, after Garett proposed, then she was told in no uncertain terms she'd be marrying Titus, she'd been in shock. She'd known her reputation was going to be hurt after she and Titus were found in bed together but she'd never imagined things would go this far.

Now, she was standing before the minister from town, ready to say vows to a man that she knew she had feelings for but who she also knew would never be able to give those feelings to her in return. Her dream of marrying for love was gone and the man before her didn't seem to care.

He'd decided on his own that he'd fix the damage that'd been done to her reputation and her brothers had been more than happy to let him.

She'd never hated being a woman more than she did at this moment, knowing that other people had the power to accuse her of something she didn't do and make her marry just to protect her good name.

The minister had been brought out from town and with the sun starting to set across the fields, she could hear his voice as he joined them in marriage.

"Ella? Do you need me to repeat the words?" The kind man put his hand on her arm. Titus was holding her hands between them and she looked down at the minister's hand, swallowing hard to keep the lump in her throat down.

"Sorry." She looked back up and met Titus's gaze. His face had a pained expression as he stood completely still waiting for her to speak. She knew how much he didn't want to marry and now he was stuck here with a wife he never wanted. He was marrying her out of a sense of obligation to right a wrong he'd never even committed. She could have laughed out loud at the absurdity of the entire situation but she was sure those who were watching would think she'd gone mad.

"I do." The words were choked out and she was almost certain she saw Titus let his breath out.

She listened as he repeated his vows to her, never taking her eyes from his. She tried not to be mad at him, knowing it wasn't his fault, but she had to be angry at someone and he was the one in front of her.

As she heard him say the words, she felt her heart skip a beat and, for a moment, she let herself believe she was being married to a man who loved her.

The next words knocked the breath from her. "You may kiss the bride." The minister looked happily between the two of them, obviously not aware of the situation that had forced them to marry.

She stood with her mouth open, unsure what to do. As she watched, a grin spread across Titus's face and before she could stop him, he was bending down to meet her lips. Just before they met, he whispered so only she could hear, "May as well make the most of it." His eyebrows lifted and dropped quickly and, before she knew it, she could feel the heat of his lips on hers.

He kissed her so gently, she was sure she could still feel air between their lips but as he kept his lips moving on hers, her heart started beating double time. A tear escaped as the emotion of the past few hours caught up to her, combined with the tender kiss Titus was giving her. For one moment, she'd been able to forget this wasn't a marriage out of necessity only.

He pulled back just enough to look in her eyes and he lifted one hand to wipe the tear away that had made its way to his lips. His other hand still held her arm, holding her close to him. "I'm sorry Ella. I wish there was another way."

She didn't want him to be nice. She needed to hold on to her anger so the feelings she knew she was starting to have for him wouldn't get crushed.

She pushed back while everyone around them cheered as though they'd just witnessed a beautiful wedding between two people in love.

Her sisters-in-law were the first ones over to her, taking her by the hand and each pulling her in for a hug.

"Ella, give it some time and I know things will work out. I see how he looks at you." Phoebe hugged her close to her fully pregnant belly, then pulled back to smile down at her.

Audrey took a turn, agreeing with Phoebe. "And, I can see how you look at him. Maybe the two of you don't realize it yet but I can see there is something there. You might still get your chance to be married for love." Audrey was beautiful and always so optimistic. She'd married her brother Reid knowing it was a marriage in name only but they'd ended up falling deeply in love.

Ella didn't hold out that same hope with Titus.

There wouldn't be any celebration for her wedding and, as she stood between Phoebe and Audrey, she had to choke back the tears that were threatening. The men who'd been working on the barn all day started making their way to their wagons like nothing out of the ordinary had just happened.

Her brothers seemed to know she was angry with them, at the moment, so were keeping their distance. She was almost able to smile as she watched them warily look her direction as they started to pack up their wagons to head home.

Garett had been angry when Titus stepped up to marry her. He hadn't said much since then and, now as she watched, she saw him glare at Titus before turning to get on his horse to head home. Something about that look caused her to shiver. As much as she wouldn't admit it, she was far happier to be married to Titus than him.

"I'll be fine. You don't need to worry about me." She tried to say the words with confidence but by the way the other two women looked at her, she knew they didn't believe her.

"Titus is a good man. At least he won't hurt you." Audrey smiled and tried to offer her reassurance.

What Audrey didn't know was that Titus already

had more power to hurt her than any of them realized.

❧

TITUS WATCHED as Ella led the horse in a circle in the pen. She held the rope tightly, not letting the horse have too much of a lead as she worked her through the moves she'd taught her.

She was angry at him and wouldn't even look his way. She'd barely spoken to him in the past two days since they were married and, when she did, she made sure to let him know how unhappy she was with the arrangement.

The barn was finished now and she'd wasted no time getting back to work with the horses, obviously relieved at not having to keep tending to the men who were working.

He was still living outside the house and had moved his belongings back into the new barn which wasn't exactly how he'd pictured a married couple would spend their first few nights together. But, he knew their marriage was far from ordinary.

He put his elbows up on the top rail and lifted a booted foot to place on the bottom rail as he watched. He knew why she was upset and he couldn't blame her. It had to be hard not having control over your future and because she was a woman, she was being forced into something she didn't want.

He felt bad but, at the time, he hadn't known what else to do.

And, he didn't want to admit how much it had bothered him to think of Garett marrying her. When the other man had offered to marry her, he'd felt a jealousy he couldn't explain.

He knew he'd acted hastily but what was done was done. And whether she liked it or not, they were married. He tried not to let himself think about his own worries and his own reasons for never wanting to marry.

The thought that he could ever lose his temper and hurt Ella like his father had done to his mother terrified him.

He needed to keep his feelings in check. And, at the moment, Ella being mad at him was exactly what he needed.

It kept him angry too, which was safer for him.

He thrust his hand through his hair, pushing his wide-brimmed hat back on his head. He was frustrated it was taking so long to find who'd caused all of these problems in the first place. It didn't make sense and, now, not only had he lost two people he cared about over a bunch of horses, he was stuck married to a woman who would most likely rather see him dead.

Ella had the horse in the pen laying down on

command, a skill that was highly sought after by the cavalry who were their largest buyers. The men would be able to command their horses to get down on the ground, offering them cover during battle.

"It's still taking too long for that horse to get down." He knew he was being ornery and, that in truth, he had no right to say anything since he couldn't train the horse himself near as well as she could. But, he was grumpy and she was right there in front of him.

She stood up, holding the rope as she commanded the horse to rise. She didn't even acknowledge that he'd spoke.

"You're giving her too much lead." Now, he knew he was just itching for a fight. He didn't know if she was giving too much lead or not.

Apparently, she was ready to give him one, the frustration and anger of the past few days catching up to her too. She stopped and stood perfectly still while the horse grunted and stomped the ground beside her. Ella's eyes locked on his and he actually felt a moment of regret knowing he was about to pay for his words.

Her split skirt moved slightly as the breeze blew it and he watched as she reached up and absently pushed back wisps of blonde hair that had fallen over her eyes. He could see her chest moving up and down beneath the vest she wore over her blouse as she struggled to win a battle with her anger he knew she would lose.

She was as sweet as apple pie most of the time but when she was mad, he'd been on the receiving end enough times to know a man should likely run for cover.

Slowly, she started walking toward where he stood leaning on the wooden fence, never letting go of the rope in her hand, forcing the horse to follow along behind her. As she got closer, he could feel himself swallow.

When she stopped right in front of him, they both just stood looking at each other without saying a word. Finally, she broke the silence.

"She's all yours."

He'd expected her to yell or at least give him some kind of argument. But instead, she handed him the rope for the horse and turned around to walk away.

Why didn't he just keep his thoughts to himself?

Now he was stuck doing something with the horse that was standing and snorting at him. He was sure even she was laughing at him. And, the worst part was, Ella hadn't even given him the fight he'd been itching for in the first place.

"What do you expect me to do with this horse? That's your job, not mine." He wasn't quite ready to let her just walk away without at least a bit of a fight.

She stopped and turned, then tilted her head to the side. "Titus, you really don't want me to answer what I'd like you to do with that horse."

He knew his mouth was gaping open, as he stood watching her walk to the barn. The dryness of the air tickled the back of his throat but, no matter how hard he tried, he couldn't think of a response.

For the first time in his life, Titus Cain was at a loss for words.

CHAPTER 13

"Oh my dear, just ignore her. She's been jealous of you since the day she arrived in town." Susan O'Hara patted her arm. She was standing in the O'Hara's mercantile and Connie McGinley had just been in with her father. They'd spent their entire time in the store staring at Ella. Douglas had even shaken his head disapprovingly in her direction as they turned to leave the store.

But, what bothered Ella the most was the subtle comment Connie had made sure she heard as she walked past.

"I can't believe she'd show up in town so soon after forcing poor Titus to marry her." She'd been walking beside her father as they left the store but Ella knew without a doubt that Connie had wanted her to hear her words.

"Besides, that woman has had her eye on Titus

since the day her family arrived in Oregon." Susan was still trying to make her feel better.

The McGinleys had arrived just a couple of months ago and Connie had soon learned who the single men were in the area. She'd had her eye on Titus, as well as Ella's brother Logan. Ella cringed knowing that now her brother better watch his back because she'd be turning her attentions to him.

Ella had felt the stares of some of the other townsfolk as they'd rode into Bethany this morning but most of the people had still been friendly and acted like nothing had happened at all. Even though Ella knew this was big news in these parts where nothing exciting ever really happened, the people who were friends with the family and who'd lived here longer, all offered her their support.

It was only the new families in town and some of the ones who'd always been more judgmental than the rest, who seemed to be intent on making things bad. In Ella's mind, these were the ones who had forced the marriage in the first place.

"I know, Susan. I have no intention of hanging my head in shame. I know what really happened between me and Titus and I have nothing to be ashamed of. If you asked me, it's the people who were calling my reputation into question in the first place who should be ashamed of themselves." Ella tried to make her voice sound more sure than she really felt, not wanting anyone to know how angry and hurt she actually was.

"And now, Titus is stuck here until we can get this all sorted. I have no intention of forcing him to stay in this marriage that happened against his will." Ella swallowed hard, hoping to keep her voice even as she felt her chin start to waver.

Susan's eyes met her's and the older woman smiled as she tilted her head sideways. "Are you so sure it was against his will, Ella?"

Ella gave a little snort of laughter. "Oh trust me, Titus never wanted to marry and least of all me. He can barely tolerate being around me for a few hours while we work, never mind having to spend the rest of his days and nights, with me too." She shook her head as she laughed out loud again.

"No, he married me out of the overbearing sense of duty he has and to fix a situation that wasn't even his fault in the first place. The marriage was most definitely against his will." She nodded her head at Susan to make sure the other woman didn't have any more doubt.

Susan just shrugged then turned to take down another bolt of fabric she wanted to show Ella.

"I don't know. Seems to me Titus Cain isn't the type of man to do anything he doesn't want to do."

Ella made sure the other woman hadn't turned back around before she rolled her eyes. Just because everyone else kept reminding her that Titus could've let Garett marry her or he could've just left things as they were and let Ella handle the ruined reputation on her own, it didn't make her believe he would have been the kind of man to do that for any other reason than his sense of duty.

And, even though more than one person had told her they were sure Titus hadn't been forced into the marriage, Ella knew better. Other than the one kiss he'd given her the night of the storm, he'd never given any other indication he even noticed she was a woman.

She knew they'd built a strong friendship and even though she was still furious with him for insisting they get married in front of everyone, making it impossible to argue, the truth was, it *had* scared her to know what others would be saying about her.

She tried to put on a brave front all the time but there were times when she wished she had someone to share in the burdens and to help fix problems as they arose. That had been one of those times.

She didn't want to be known as the "fallen woman" around town, with people whispering behind her back. And even though she was angry that he hadn't given her any say in the matter, her heart had secretly done somersaults when Titus had said he'd marry her.

Even if it was for all the wrong reasons.

As Susan finished putting all of her purchases

together, the bell above the door jingled, announcing someone coming into the store. Ella turned and felt her heart miss a beat as she watched Titus walk through the door.

She knew her heart was hopelessly lost to this man which was only going to cause her pain. If Walter had ever known the trouble they'd be in because of him leaving his farm to the two of them, he'd have felt terrible.

She knew it would be up to her to figure a way out of the mess they were in.

"Are you ladies all finished up or still ear wagging?" He offered them both a smile and Ella noticed Susan come out from behind the desk to walk over and hug Titus. She almost laughed at the expression of confusion on his face as the older woman embraced him.

"Congratulations on your marriage to this sweet, young girl here." Ella could feel her cheeks start to burn. What was Susan doing? She knew the circumstances about their marriage and they'd just been talking about how he'd been forced into it.

"You take good care of her. You're lucky to have a woman like her who is willing to work alongside you like she does to take care of that farm." Susan was nodding her head as she pulled back and patted him on his arm.

Titus was still staring down at the woman with his mouth half open.

Ella decided it was time to get them both out of there to avoid any further embarrassment.

Grabbing everything in her arms, she bolted toward the doorway, almost knocking Titus down as she went past. "Thanks for everything, Susan. I'll see you next time I'm in town."

She caught the smile on Susan's face as she went past and noticed her wink at Titus. She was glad to hear him say his goodbyes and follow her to the door, pushing it open for her to get through.

When they got out onto the wooden walkway, she felt herself let out the breath she'd been holding. She loved Susan like a second mother but the woman sure knew how to embarrass her.

"Well, at least one person is happy about our marriage." Titus reached over and took the load of items she was carrying into his arms. He grinned down at her before continuing on past her, leaving her standing there watching his back as he bent down and set everything into the wagon.

"Yes, well Susan has some romantic notions in her head that everything will all work out and we'll live happily ever after. She doesn't know the truth." Ella was annoyed. Why was everyone else acting so nonchalant about her marriage?

Of all people, Titus should be just as annoyed. Instead, he seemed to be enjoying her discomfort and was fine with people believing there was more to their marriage than there really was.

Titus turned and opened his mouth to respond, but before he could speak, Henry Carson rode up on his horse, leaving a cloud of dust to settle down around them as he hopped down beside him. Ella braced herself, knowing how much Titus hated the man.

"Well, well, well. I just had to stop and see if the rumors were true. Did you get yourself hitched, Titus Cain?" Henry's voice lifted in laughter. "I heard you'd got yourself caught in a scandalous situation and were forced to wed." Henry turned to face her.

"And you were the lucky gal who caught him." The man was enjoying taunting them with the stories he'd heard.

"What happened between me and Ella is none of your concern, Henry." Titus had his fists clenched tightly as he spat his words out between gritted teeth.

The other man wasn't done. His laughter made her skin crawl.

"So I guess now that you got yourself a man and you've forced him to stay, you won't be needing to sell your farm." Henry was sneering in her direction. "Shoulda' known you'd do something like this instead of just selling it to me."

Ella could feel herself shaking with anger.

"I didn't do anything to force Titus to stay and, I

assure you, I didn't need him in order keep that farm anyway."

Even as she said it, she couldn't help but wonder how many other people were thinking the same thing.

Henry just continued laughing, drawing attention from other people as they passed by. "You wanted to prove you could take care of that farm. You could've easily sold it to me, and been done with all of it, but instead you chose to be stubborn. Now you've gone and forced a man to stick with you to help just so you won't lose it." Henry was shaking his head as he laughed.

Before she knew what was happening, Titus had Henry by the scruff of his shirt. He lifted the other man off the ground, letting his feet dangle as he pulled him up close.

"Ella never forced me into anything I didn't want. And, she wouldn't have had to anyway. Half that farm was mine. I wasn't going anywhere." Titus's cheeks were fiery red and she could see the muscles in his arms trembling under his tight shirt as he held the other man in front of him.

"What do you mean? Why would half the farm be yours?" Henry's voice came out on a choked whisper as his airway was being closed in the grip Titus had on him.

Ella watched as Titus sneered in Henry's face. "Because Walter Jenkins was my uncle and I was never going anywhere until I proved you killed him and my brother."

Ella gasped at the same time as Henry. Why would Titus have told him now after all this time? Now Henry would know who to watch out for and he would make sure to cover his tracks. After everything they'd been through to find the proof they needed, Titus had just thrown that away.

Not to mention the fact that now Titus was in danger too.

"My reasons for marrying Ella have nothing to do with her trapping me here and, like I said before, they're no concern of yours. You'll never get that land. I'll make sure of that. Now, I'm going to set you down and you're going to turn and walk away before I do something I'll regret."

He lowered the other man to the ground while Ella still stood in shock as she watched Henry reach up and rub his neck. "You're crazy." Henry started to back away toward his horse. "I want that land. I've never made any secret of that but I never killed Walter. Or anyone else."

Henry put his foot in the stirrup and swung his leg up on his horse. "But you better watch your back because once it gets out that you have a stake in that land, you could end up the same as your uncle." He turned to look at her, squinting his eyes as he lifted a corner of his lip. "You could be a widow before you even have a chance to enjoy being a wife."

With his words echoing in her ears, she watched as Henry rode away. She could feel the blood rushing from her face as she understood how true his words were.

Titus was now a target. And, making it even worse, she realized how terrified she was of losing him.

CHAPTER 14

T he ride back from town had been quiet and Titus had looked over at Ella more than once to try and gauge her mood. She was upset he had no doubt about that. She'd sat as stiff as the seat she was sitting on and hadn't even argued with him once.

He unhitched the horses, then set them out to graze while he lifted the supplies from the wagon. Ella hadn't even waited for him to help her down. She was already in the house changing into her split skirt so she could work with the horses. He wasn't sure how long they'd be able to work outside today because the skies were starting to turn as dark as his mood.

He found himself absently looking around for Wally. The mule was always under his feet it seemed but he didn't see him around anywhere. Maybe he was hiding somewhere knowing a storm was coming. Titus wasn't sure who was more afraid of storms, the mule or Ella, but he thought back to the last storm that had caused so much havoc in his life.

The kiss he'd shared with Ella still burned his lips whenever he thought about it which he hated to admit was often. And, making it worse, was the fact that now she was his wife and he should be able to enjoy kissing her whenever he wanted.

But, he knew she wasn't ready to make it a real marriage. And, the truth was, he didn't know what he wanted either. All he knew was that now he had no intentions of going back home. He was going to stay here and he hoped he could somehow prove to himself and Ella that he could be a better man than his father had been.

It was a fear that still consumed him. Even though he hadn't ever acted in the way his father did, he still had worries that someday he'd end up just like him.

And, he knew Ella deserved better than that.

He peeked into the barn to see if he could see the mule hiding in the back where the hay was kept. Not seeing any sign of him, he continued walking up to the house with the supplies. He braced himself, knowing he was going to have to tell Ella he couldn't find Wally. She'd become far too attached to that animal.

Kicking the door open with his foot, he stopped

dead in his tracks when Ella whipped around holding her shirt in front of her. "Can't you ever knock?"

He felt like the wind had been knocked out of him as he stood staring at the woman in front of him. Her blond hair tumbled around her shoulders, obviously not withstanding having the dress she'd been wearing pulled over her head.

She was putting on the frilly tan blouse she wore with her split skirt. But, she was standing before him in just her underthings, and Titus didn't know which way to look. His body was screaming not to move but he knew it wasn't right to be standing there ogling Ella, even if she was his wife.

"Well, the way you ran from the wagon, I wasn't sure where you'd even gone. We have supplies that need putting away or did you forget?" He wasn't sure why he was still standing facing her. He couldn't stop his eyes from taking it all in, the long legs that were peeking out behind the shirt she was using to block herself, and the curved hips that weren't quite hidden behind the edges of the fabric.

His eyes moved up and met hers and he was sure he could feel fire burning into his own. This was a dangerous position to be standing in. Deciding to take the easy way out, he turned his back to let her finish dressing. He was still holding the supplies in his arms and they'd suddenly become a whole lot heavier than he remembered.

"I didn't forget. I just assumed you could carry them on your own without needing my help. I need to get to work with the horses before the storm sets in." He could hear the rustling of fabric behind him as she hurried to get dressed.

"And besides, this is my house and I would appreciate it if you didn't just come traipsing in here as you want without even considering my privacy."

He turned back around, setting the supplies onto the small table as he put a booted foot up onto the chair beside him. He laughed to himself as she frantically worked to do up the buttons. "Well, as I remember it, I was left half of this farm too, which would include the house. Now that we're married, I have just as much right to be in this house." He paused to make sure his next words were heard.

"And, your bed if we're being completely honest."

He heard her gasp and watched as her cheeks turned a fiery shade of red. Her fists tightened as her jaw clenched and her eyes squinted into slits. "You better not even try, Titus Cain."

She was breathing fast, her chest rising and falling as she eyed him up. What was it about Ella that made him want to grab her in his arms and kiss her until she couldn't stand but at the same time, make him itch for a fight with her?

He dropped his foot from the chair and walked toward her. Her fingers were still holding the button she'd been working on, and he reached out and took hold of it, pushing it through the hole to do it up. He moved up to the next button and continued until he reached the top.

He could feel her throat move as she swallowed and he suddenly felt his throat go as dry as the dirt floor he stood on.

His fingers brushed her neck and he heard her take a breath. "Ella, what have you done to me?" He felt his head lower and he knew he should stop himself before it was too late but, like a moth to a flame, he was helpless to resist.

His lips found hers as his arms went behind her to pull her closer to him. He hoped she would push him away, making it easier for him to stop, but when he felt her arms go around him, he knew he was lost. His mouth opened hers and his hands moved up to entwine in her hair. He heard himself groan low in his throat and he knew he had to stop himself.

He'd never force himself on a woman like his father had done.

Like water had been poured over his head, he pulled back. When he looked into Ella's eyes, he noticed that instead of the usual bright blue, they were so dark he was sure they were black.

He struggled to get his breathing back under control while neither of them said a word, holding each other and keeping their eyes locked.

"I'm sorry, Ella. I didn't mean to do that." He wasn't sure why he was apologizing but he never wanted to make a woman feel he'd forced himself on her.

He noticed her chin start to tremble. But, she swallowed hard, loud enough for the sound to reach his ears, then pulled herself out of his arms. She brought her arms up and hugged herself as she turned from him.

Reaching out, he grabbed her arm so she couldn't move further away.

"Ella, we need to talk. We need to figure out what's going to happen here. With us." He couldn't keep going on like this.

She whipped around, and he noticed the color back in her cheeks and the blue in her eyes. "What's to figure out, Titus? We ended up having to get married, something neither of us ever wanted. I wanted to marry for love. I wanted a man who could see me as their equal, as a partner, and someone they could love beyond reason. I know it's crazy but that's all I've ever wanted." She was blinking fast, fighting against tears that were threatening to fall.

"Instead, I'm married to a man who never wanted to marry me and only did it because he felt like he had to fix something. Who never thought to discuss it with me first to see if it was the only solution. And who plans to leave, and go back home, leaving me alone without the chance of ever finding anyone who could give me what I wanted."

Her voice was strangled and each word tore at his chest.

She moved to walk past him, but he held her arm.

"Ella..."

She ripped her arm from his grasp. She looked up at him with eyes now wet with tears. "No, Titus. We don't have anything else to talk about. Henry was right and so is everyone else who is whispering about us. You were forced to marry me, against your will, and now we're both stuck here in a marriage we didn't want. And there's nothing we can do to fix it." She stood in front of him, trembling. He wanted to reach out and take her in his arms but he knew he didn't have the right.

"Then, you go and tell Henry the truth about you and this farm. Don't you realize that now you are in even more danger than before? Whoever wants this land, and we both know exactly who that is, isn't going to sit back now and wait. They are going to get rid of you, leaving me to fight on my own to keep the farm. Unless they decide to just get rid of me too..." Her voice choked and he couldn't take it anymore. He pulled her into his arms.

"Ella, is that what has you so worked up today? What Henry said?" He didn't wait for her to answer, knowing full well he wouldn't get one. "I'm not going anywhere. I meant that. Henry can make all the threats he wants, I'm not that easy to get rid of. I'd have thought you'd know that by now."

She pulled back, wiping at her eyes with the back of her hand.

"I have to get to work before the storm gets here." She lifted her eyes to his. "Working with those horses is the only thing I still have any control over."

With those words, she turned and walked out the door.

He was left standing, watching her back as she made her way to the barn. He reached up and lifted his hat, brushing his hand through his hair as he realized, after all that, he'd never even told her about Wally.

☙❧

ELLA DROPPED the rope she was holding, unable to stop her hands from shaking.

Her nerves were stretched as tight as they could go today already then, when Titus had walked in on her getting dressed, she'd been unable to move.

The kiss they'd shared had left her entire body trembling and she'd realized, at that moment, she was in love with the man who was holding her in his arms. The man who'd infuriated her since the day he arrived, who'd argued and questioned everything she did. The same one who'd never once questioned her ability to work with the horses or to take over the care of the farm they shared.

When the realization had hit her, she thought the world had dropped out from under her. She was married to the man she loved but she was sure he didn't love her back. Every time he kissed her, he apologized and said he shouldn't have done it. Obviously, the feelings she had weren't shared.

How could she have been so foolish? Now, when everything was finally settled, her heart would be left in pieces. Titus would go back home and she'd never know what it felt like to have a man love her in return.

She was terrified that Henry would hurt Titus now.

A loud crack of thunder caused her to jump. She'd only just started working with the mare and as she lifted her eyes to the sky, she realized the storm had moved in fast while she was lost in her thoughts. She watched Titus walk toward the pen and felt her heart do the familiar double beat.

"Have you seen Wally?" Ella looked to either side, suddenly remembering she hadn't seen the mule at all since they'd got home. She'd been so caught up in her own problems, she hadn't noticed he was missing.

"No, isn't he around back?" She knew he sometimes liked to hide behind the barn in a clump of straw he'd lay in.

She sensed something was wrong though. Titus wouldn't normally worry too much about Wally, so for him to be asking, he must have noticed him missing too.

Titus just shook his head. "I haven't seen him since before we left for town this morning."

Her heart sunk as she realized she hadn't either.

Wally was terrified of storms and if he was out there, he'd be scared. She had to find him.

She jumped up on Storm's back and kicked her heels into the mare's sides. "What are you doing?" Titus's voice reached her ears as she raced past him out of the paddock. He tried to grab the reins that were hanging down but she was too far away.

"I'm going to find him." She heard him curse loudly as she flew out of the yard. As she rode away, his voice bellowed behind her.

"Not without me, you aren't."

CHAPTER 15

"Ella! Are you trying to get yourself killed?" She could hear the pounding of the hooves as Titus caught up to her. His voice thundered above the wind that was starting to blow around them as the storm rolled in.

She let her mare have her lead and smiled to herself despite the worries consuming her. Riding her horses was the one thing that always could make her smile. As her hair flew in the wind behind her, she tipped her head back and enjoyed the cool air hitting her face.

Suddenly, she could feel the push of another horse riding up alongside her and she knew the moment Titus reached over and grabbed the reins to pull her in.

"Just because you want to get away from me, you

don't need to go hell-bent out into a storm on your own. Not to mention the fact there is someone out here who'd be more than happy to get rid of you so there'd be one less obstacle in their way to getting this land." His voice roared in her ears and, as she thought back, she realized it was the first time she'd ever heard him shout that loud.

He'd hollered and argued loudly many times but his voice was different this time. He was furious.

She felt the first drops of rain hit her face as she stared at the man on the horse beside her. The wind was picking up and the storm around them seemed to echo the feelings between them.

The sound of a loud whinny reached her ears. She knew it was Wally by the strange sound the mule made which wasn't quite a bray like a donkey, but not a true whinny like a horse. He had a sound all his own.

And, her heart lurched as she realized how scared he must be.

She leaped from her horse's back and ran toward the sound. Titus was right behind her. He grabbed her arm. "Stay put. I will go in and get him." They'd reached a thick bush that sat next to the creek. The water in the creek was rushing past, filling up fast as the rain fell hard around them.

"Hold the horses." He thrust the reins from his horse into her hands, then pushed aside the first branches. Ella's heart stopped as she saw the poor mule standing out on a broken tree laying across the bank of the creek. The water was starting to rise and Wally didn't know which way to go.

Titus eased his way closer, talking loud enough for Wally to hear his voice as he offered soothing words. She knew Titus grumbled about Wally constantly but she could also tell he had a soft spot for the mule even if he'd never admit it to her.

She was sure the strong and powerful Titus Cain would deny ever caring about a mule.

But, the way he was coaxing Wally and talking to him to keep him calm, warmed her heart. Titus was unlike any man she'd ever known. Her brothers were strong and she knew they had a soft side but she didn't see it often.

Titus had a side of him that most people would never believe. Working with him over the past few months had shown her what a good man he was even if he tried to let on otherwise.

"It's all right old boy. Just stay there. I've almost got you." Wally's eyes weren't leaving Titus and his nostrils were flaring from his fear. Titus reached out but his foot slipped on the bank. Ella screamed as he started to slide, her hand flying to cover her mouth as she saw him catch a shrub to stop his fall.

It had scared Wally enough that he'd started to move when he saw Titus fall and Ella was sure if he'd gone in, Wally would have jumped in after him.

Whether Titus liked it or not, Wally had a strong affection for him.

Finally, Titus was able to edge out far enough to get his hand near Wally. The mule snorted and walked closer to his hand, then kept moving closer until Titus could get his hands around his neck. Once Wally realized he was safe, he bounded up the bank toward Ella. He stuck his head in under her arm, pushing at her to pet him.

"What were you doing Wally? How did you get out here on your own?" She rubbed the mule behind the ears as another burst of lightning came from the sky. The thunder that followed shook the ground and Wally started to bolt. Luckily, Titus had got back over to them and got an arm around his neck before he could get far.

"No, you don't. We're all heading back to that outcropping of rocks I saw a ways back and getting out of this storm." He had to shout over the sound of the rain beating down around them. The water was pouring off the front of his hat, and Ella realized they were both soaked right through their clothes.

He grabbed his horse, still keeping one hand on Wally's neck who was following right on his heels. Ella grabbed her horse and they all moved as fast as they could behind Titus, the wind whipping her hair into her eyes and the rain hitting her hard on the face.

The ground was soft, making it hard to keep up with Titus. She was having a hard time seeing where she was going as the rain pelted down and, suddenly, her leg collapsed beneath her as her foot stumbled over something on the ground.

She tried to get back up but her heavy skirts were weighing her down, making it difficult to maneuver. Her heart was pounding so loud she could hear it echoing in her ears over the sound of the wind and rain around her. She was terrified.

Titus must have realized she wasn't behind him and she felt herself give a cry of relief when she saw him coming toward her. He reached down, water dripping off his hat onto her blouse, and lifted her up against his chest.

"Are you all right?" He looked down at her waiting for her to respond, brushing the wet hair back from her face.

"I'm fine. I just slipped." But, she wasn't taking any chances that he'd set her back down. She wanted out of this storm as fast as possible and she knew her best odds were in his arms being carried. She threw her arms around his neck, and he turned to head back the direction he'd been going.

They walked for what seemed like hours but Ella was sure was only a few minutes before they reached the rocks Titus had mentioned. They formed a small cave that would give them some shelter out of the rain. It was big enough for the horses and Wally to get inside too.

He gently set her down, then plopped onto the ground beside her. He was breathing hard and she could see his shoulders moving as he worked to catch his breath.

"I'm sorry, Titus. I could've walked the rest of the way." She felt bad knowing he had to carry her, all while fighting against the swirling wind and rain around him.

He looked at her sideways while he reached up and took his wet hat from his head. His hair was soaked beneath it, and her heart gave a flutter in her chest as she saw the curls that had formed in his hair. He pushed his hands through the thick hair, wringing out drops of water onto the ground beside him.

"I'm sure you could've but, frankly, I was tired of getting soaked through. I wasn't inclined to wait for you to drag your heavy skirts any longer." He was unbuttoning his shirt now.

"What are you doing?" Her voice came out as a high pitched squeak.

He stopped and looked at her with one eyebrow quirked. "Getting out of my wet clothes. I'm not about to get pneumonia on account of a mule who decided to wander off in the middle of a storm." Wally seemed to sense he was being talked about, so he came over and pushed against Titus with his nose.

"Get off me, you flea-bitten bag of bones." Titus pushed Wally away but the mule just decided to lay down beside him.

"Well, the storm seems to be letting up a bit so, if you don't mind, I'd rather you just stay dressed. We've already been caught in one compromising situation; I don't need anyone finding us out here with you undressed." She tried to keep her voice from showing how nervous she was suddenly feeling.

He sat staring at her, then shook his head as he let his hands drop from the buttons. "I'm pretty sure no one would question anything since we're married now or did you forget that?"

"How could I forget that? I'm reminded of it everywhere we go." She didn't mean for it to come out sounding so sad.

Titus kept his gaze on her for a moment, then sighed loudly as he looked down at the ground between his folded legs. Drops of water fell from his hair. "Is it really that distasteful being married to me? Would you rather I let people talk about your ruined reputation, whispering behind your back every time you showed your face in town?" He looked back up at her. "Or, would you rather I'd just let Garett Jackson marry you?"

She felt terrible as she looked at him and realized he'd genuinely done what he believed was best for her. But, she'd been acting like a spoiled child who hadn't got her way.

She needed to let him know she was sorry and that she did appreciate everything he'd done for her. He'd given up his own freedom to be able to leave and go back home when he married her.

"I'm sorry, Titus. I know you did it for me and now you're stuck here being married when you never wanted to get married in the first place." They sat looking at each other as the thunder echoed in the distance. Rain drops could be heard splashing as they hit the rocks around them. He just sat without saying anything, making her uncomfortable. "Why didn't you ever want to get married anyway? You never did tell me. You've always just been so adamant that you'd never be married. Was there a woman who hurt you?"

He lifted an eyebrow as he looked at her. "Do I look like the kind of man who'd let a woman cause me any kind of trouble? I've never let a woman get close enough to hurt me."

She rolled her eyes. "So the mighty Titus Cain can't be hurt by a woman. All right, so what happened to make you so against getting married?"

He didn't say anything for a while, the sound of Wally snoring beside them the only thing that could be heard above the quiet falling of the rain as it eased.

"Oh, even I could be hurt by a woman, make no mistake about that." The huskiness in his voice caused her whole body to tremble. "But that's not why I wanted to keep myself from wedded bliss." He looked out toward the opening of the rocks.

She didn't think he was going to continue speaking.

"My mother was the most beautiful and kind woman I've ever known in my life. She'd have done anything for the people she loved, especially me, my brother and my little sister."

"I never knew you had a sister. I've never heard you mention her." She worried he might not continue now that she'd interrupted but, when she looked at him, she realized he was lost in another place and time and was ready to tell her everything.

"My father, on the other hand, was a horrible man. He only cared about himself. Walter had raised my ma after her parents were killed and I know it hurt him terribly to watch how my father treated her. He tried so many times to get her away from him but she wouldn't go. She was loyal to the man she'd married."

He leaned back against the rocks. "When they'd married, Walter had given some of the family land to them so they could have a good start. But, my pa never wanted to be a farmer. He had bigger plans. He needed more money so, after a few years of just getting by, he sold just about everything he could and decided to gamble to get more money. When that didn't happen, and he lost everything, he spent the next few years drinking and blaming everyone around him for what happened."

She watched as his eyes squinted and his jaw clenched tightly as he remembered.

"My ma took the worst of it. She tried to protect us but when he got drinking, he was mean. I know that's why Walter moved out here at his age, hoping he could get something set up so he could convince her to get far away from him."

He swallowed hard and she found herself reaching her hand out to put on his arm, sensing he was recalling something he didn't want to remember.

"I never told my brother or Walter, or anyone for that matter, about the time I came in and caught him hurting my ma in a way no woman should ever be hurt. That day, I beat him until he was almost dead. I wanted to kill him but my ma begged me to stop. A few days later, she came down with a sickness and she didn't have the strength to fight it. He killed her as sure as if he'd put his hands around her throat and squeezed."

Her heart clenched as she imagined what he'd witnessed.

"After that, I spent my time keeping my sister and my brother safe. And, my father spent his days telling me I was just like him. He said he'd seen the fury in my eyes when I'd beat him that day and he enjoyed talking about how I'd someday treat my wife just like he had and that I was no better than him."

"Titus, you would never do that! I've known you long enough to know you'd never hurt anyone, especially someone you cared about." She had no doubt in her mind.

He looked at her with eyes that were black from the memories he was living. "My pa told me he'd been just like me. He never thought he'd be like he was either but he said it was in our blood. That's how his pa had been with his own mother."

The sorrow in his voice tore at her chest. She wanted to comfort him and moved closer. But, before she could get there, his eyes moved past her to something behind her. "What's that?" His voice was back to normal as he moved to reach for whatever he'd seen.

She turned and saw him pull a piece of fabric out from between some rocks she'd been sitting in front of. The rocks moved and a dusty vest came out of the rubble.

"This is Martin's." His voice was low as he rubbed his hands over the fabric and she could see the sorrow in his eyes as he realized this was something that'd belonged to his brother. As he moved his hands, they stopped over the pocket, then reached inside.

He pulled out a piece of paper and slowly opened it with trembling hands. Ella watched as his eyes darkened again and his shoulders started to move as his breathing became heavier.

He lifted his eyes to her as he crumpled the paper in his hands. "I'm going to kill him."

CHAPTER 16

Titus was on his horse and racing away before she even had a chance to say another word. He'd taken the crumpled paper with him, so she didn't even know what it was he'd read. Obviously, his brother had found shelter in this same small cave of rocks at one time and she could only assume by Titus's reaction that it'd been shortly before his death.

She knew Titus was on his way to Henry Carson's, so she needed to find someone to go with her to make sure he didn't do anything drastic. After what he'd just told her, she knew without a doubt he'd never forgive himself if he let his temper take control of him. Even if it was to make someone pay for what they'd done to his brother.

She managed to get Wally up and moving and was now making her way back home with just a drizzle of rain coming down. Thankfully, for both her and Wally's sake, the storm had passed.

She saw a lone figure on a horse making its way toward her. Recognizing her brother Logan, she raced Storm toward him. "Logan, Titus has gone off all hell-bent for revenge on Henry. He found some piece of paper in a pocket of his brother's vest and he ran off saying he was going to kill him..." Her words were running all together as she tried to catch her breath and explain it all to her brother.

"Whoa Ella! Slow down, you aren't making any sense." Logan grabbed Storm's reins as the mare paced around his horse, sensing Ella's distress. "What are you talking about?"

"Titus. We were caught in the storm in a small cave just back there." She flung her arm in the direction she'd just came from, where they could see Wally still loping toward them.

She swallowed hard and took a deep breath. She knew they didn't have any time to waste, so she needed to explain everything.

"We found a vest that'd been his brother's. There was a piece of paper in the vest. I don't know what it said, all I know is that after he read it, Titus raced out of there saying he was going to kill him. He's going to Henry's, I just know it! We have to stop him before he gets hurt." The last words came out as a sob as the full reality of what could happen hit her.

The man she loved could be killed.

"If he was going to Henry's, I would have met him Ella. I've just come back from town. I was caught in the storm but just kept making my way slowly this direction. I stopped at your place but didn't see anyone there, so I kept going and headed for home."

"But, if you didn't see him, where did he go?" She was confused, her mind a whirlwind of thoughts as she tried to figure out where he'd gone.

"Well, I don't know. I was talking to Henry in town today Ella. He told me something I wanted to tell you and Titus. That's why I came this way first."

Her brother pulled his hat off his head and gave it a hard shake to get rid of the water that was dripping from it. The rain had finally stopped and the sun was already starting to peak back out from behind the clouds.

"He said you had a run-in this morning in town and something Titus said made him think. He knew Walter had been killed but he hadn't known Martin had been killed too. He said he realized he should likely tell you why Walter's land has been so valuable, so you could stop this before anyone else got killed."

"But I thought Henry was the one Titus said wants the land?" None of what her brother was saying was making any sense.

"He said he does want the land. He also said he

thought he was the only one who knew there was gold on the land but he knows now that someone else has found out too."

"Gold?" Surely she hadn't heard him right. Walter had never said anything about gold.

"Walter hadn't even known there was gold on his land. Henry found it years back but before he could lay his claim, Walter had arrived and staked his claim for the land. Henry had been biding his time until he could buy the land from Walter but he says he'd never have killed anyone to get it."

Her brother focused his bright blue eyes on hers. "He said to think about who'd have the most to gain from getting their hands on this land. He said he wasn't going to tell tales on anyone unless he had proof but he said, if we were to think about it, we'd see who was behind everything - the horse thefts, the barn burning and even the deaths of Walter and Martin."

Ella couldn't think straight. "But who?" Her heart was racing and she was sure it was about to beat right out of her chest. They had to figure it out.

Garett Jackson.

Her brother must have figured it out at the exact same moment as he said the man's name out loud.

The man who'd tried to force her into marriage. The man who was the first to show up after the fire to offer his hand to help. And, the one who Walter had looked on as a friend.

Her stomach felt like it had been kicked by a horse. How could they all have been so blind?

Somehow, Garett knew there was gold on this land and since his land bordered theirs, she was sure he'd found out and decided he wanted it all.

And now, Titus was on his way there to confront him.

"I have to catch up to Titus!" She swung her horse around, ripping the reins from her brother's hands. She heard him curse loudly.

"Ella, wait! You can't go racing out there like a banshee. You'll get both of you killed."

She could hear him yelling and then the pounding of hooves behind her. She'd known there was no way her brother would let her go on her own but she also knew he wouldn't have let her go at all if she didn't get away first.

Tears were building in her eyes as she thought about Titus. She prayed to herself as they thundered across the land toward Garett's.

"Please Lord, don't let me be too late."

TITUS TRIED to rein in his anger, knowing it would cloud his judgment and he could end up putting himself in danger. But, he'd never felt fury like he did right now. The man they'd all treated as a friend was the one who'd killed both his brother and then his uncle. And, he'd tried to marry Ella knowing full well if he did, he'd finally have the land he'd already killed for.

The thought that Ella could've been in the hands of that madman caused his entire body to flush with heat.

The paper he'd found in the pocket of his brother's vest was stuffed into his own pocket. The words that he'd read left no doubt they'd all been duped by the man who lived next to Walter all these years.

The piece of paper was a map showing a vein of gold that started just on the edge of Garett's property and ran fully into Walter's.

Titus didn't know what the whole story was but he knew enough to know Garett wanted his land for the gold. And, he'd killed to get it.

He tore up the ground to Garett's, his anger mounting with every pounding of the hooves on the ground beneath him.

As he approached the house, he saw the man walking out from his barn with his hand up shielding his eyes to see who was riding toward him. It took every ounce of strength he had to stop himself from letting the horse barrel over top of the man.

"Titus! What in the sam hill are you tearing in here like that for? What's got into you?" Titus leaped from his horse's back before it'd even stopped fully and walked toward Garett with his fists clenched at his sides.

Garett's eyes practically bulged from their sockets as he realized that Titus was there for him. He started backing away and Titus could see his throat move as he swallowed.

"Do you want to tell me why you've been stealing my uncle's horses, then why you killed my brother and Walter, a man who called you a friend? Or, should I just beat it out of you? Because to be honest, the way I'm feeling right now, it would give me a great amount of satisfaction to see you laying at my feet begging for mercy."

"Titus, listen. I never meant for anyone to get killed."

He moved in closer to Garett. "So, you admit you killed them." His voice growled and he could tell by the sweat coming on the other man's brow that he was terrified.

"Let me explain."

Titus took deep breaths, trying to get his fury under control. He could see his father's laughing face every time he had the urge to swing at Garett. He knew if he didn't stop himself, he'd kill the man in front of him.

"I don't have time for listening to your sorry excuses. You're coming with me and I'm taking you down to Skinner's Mudhole where the law can deal with you."

Garett had backed up to the doorway of his barn and, as Titus watched, he saw the man's eyes change from fear to rage. The whites in his eyes grew larger and the veins on his neck stood out. Before he had a chance to react, the man pulled a pistol from just inside the door and aimed it at his heart.

His eyes squinted as he sneered at Titus.

"No one's taking me anywhere. That land is mine. I've waited long enough to get it and now you're the only thing standing in my way."

Titus needed to think. He knew he could overpower the smaller man but with a gun pointed at him, he couldn't be sure it wouldn't go off first.

"How'd you know there was gold on the land?" He needed answers. Since Garett believed he'd already won, he was more than willing to share.

"I stumbled across some gold one day, a couple years ago, down by the creek that led onto Walter's property. I worked my way back from where I found it but only found small pieces here and there. The gold came in larger amounts the closer I got to the property line. So, I decided to head into Oregon City to find out if there were any maps that would show the potential gold veins in the area." He shook his head as he continued.

"I found a business man who seemed to understand how the gold would be situated and who'd been in the area himself before it became heavily populated. He said he knew about this particular vein of gold and told me he would provide a map that would show where most of it would be." Titus watched as he clenched his jaw.

"But, then he also told me he'd tell everyone else, including Walter, if I didn't pay him. I promised him a cut when I got the land in return for his silence. He kept sending me letters and I guess your brother must have found something that sent him to visit the man in Oregon City. I've already sent him a great deal of money to keep him from telling any of you anything."

He moved closer to Titus. "But now I don't need to pay him anything else. There's no one left between me and that land. Ella will be a widow, I'll come to the rescue, and that land will all be mine." Garett's nostrils flared as his voice continued to rise.

He needed to do something now to make sure Ella wasn't left to deal with Garett on her own.

As if the mere thought of her could bring her to him, he suddenly heard the pounding of hooves and he knew even without looking it was Ella riding up behind him. He sighed inwardly, watching a grin spread across Garett's face as he looked behind Titus. He let out a laugh that stood the hair up on Titus's neck.

"Looks like your wife has decided to come and witness your death."

Why couldn't that woman just once stay put and not come charging in where she didn't belong?

"Garett, put the gun down. You're outnumbered and I'm not just going to let you gun Titus down in front of me." Logan's voice startled Titus. At least she had the good sense to find one of her brothers to come with her.

Garett just shrugged. "I can take my chances. As long as I get rid of him, I'll be happy." He thrust the gun closer to Titus as he spoke. "I couldn't believe my luck when you decided to tarnish poor Ella's reputation, forcing the need for a man to marry her. Not only would I get my hands on the land I wanted but I'd have myself the wife I'd always wanted too. The same woman who'd already turned me down once thinking she was better than me."

Now he was sneering up at Ella, who was still sitting on her horse. "I never said I was better than you, Garett. You knew I would only marry for love."

Garett's eyes were darting between all of them as he let out a loud laugh. "For love. You're such a foolish girl. You didn't seem to have any trouble marrying Titus without being in love." He practically spat his name.

"I did marry for love, Garett." Titus heard her say the words and felt his heart lurch. He was sure she was only saying it to try and reason with the man. But, it still warmed him to hear her say it.

"Ha! You don't know what love is. How could you love a man who'd lie to you about who he is? Did you know he was Walter Jenkins nephew?" He thought he was sharing information that would turn Ella against him. *How had he found that out anyway?* He had only told Henry Carson this morning and no one else knew yet.

"I knew. I also know that him and I both own the land you want." Titus knew that Ella was wasting her time reasoning with Garett. The man's eyes had lost any sense of sanity he had left.

"It's funny how easily people are bought. I was able to easily find out from old Harper in town what Walter's final will stated. I couldn't figure out how to get to you. It seemed everything I was doing kept backfiring. I knew everyone said you owned the land but I couldn't understand how. I just didn't believe a woman would be able to hold land on her own. And, I guess I was right, wasn't I, Titus?" Titus felt his stomach drop as he realized what all Garett had found out. And now Ella would know too.

"Does Ella know that she only actually has a small stake in the land and that the main title has gone to you?" Garett was enjoying watching the distress he was causing.

"It doesn't matter. Walter wanted her to have half but he knew it would be difficult for her to hold on to it with the laws about women owning their own property. He trusted me to make sure she had all she needed." He was saying the words for Ella, hoping she'd understand.

He risked turning enough to look at her. She sat completely still on her horse, looking out past the barn as she clenched her jaw tight. She finally looked down at him. "What does he mean, Titus?"

"Nothing, Ella. Don't listen to him. That land is as much yours as it is mine."

Garett must have realized he had something here that could potentially cause even more problems. "Didn't he tell you, Ella? Walter left him the majority of the land. And, now that he managed to get you married to him, he owns it all. Surely you knew that once you were hitched, anything you owned would go to your husband."

Titus glared at Garett, and if he hadn't had a gun pointed at him, he would've knocked the man to the ground.

As the thought occurred to him, he suddenly saw a blur out of the corner of his eye and he watched as Garett fell to the ground beneath a flurry of fur and hooves.

Wally had arrived and wasted no time throwing himself on the man who'd been so intent on watching Titus, he hadn't even heard Wally coming toward him.

Titus grabbed the gun as it flew out of the man's hand, then turned and watched as Ella rode away.

He had to explain to her. He needed to hear her say she loved him again. But he was afraid he'd missed his chance.

Now, she believed he'd lied to her about owning the land. She believed he'd betrayed her. And, knowing Ella, she'd believe he'd married her just to get all of the land.

Logan hopped down from his horse and took the gun from his hand. He patted him on the shoulder. "Go after her. I can take care of Garett."

Titus looked over and saw that Wally was still standing on top of the man on the ground, as Logan walked over and tied his arms together with some rope laying outside the barn.

He leaped onto his horse's back and rode after her. When he caught her, he'd make her listen whether she wanted to or not.

It was time to make sure she knew he loved her too.

CHAPTER 17

Ella could hear his voice shouting behind her and the sound of the hooves thundering across the ground as he started to catch up. She looked ahead and caught the sun starting to descend behind the hills in the distance, leaving an orange glow on the land for as far as she could see.

This land that she'd believed was hers. The land she thought had given her independence.

It had never truly been hers.

Titus had needed her to believe it was hers so he could get her out here. She tried not to let her heart believe he'd always intended to get his hands on all of the land but, right now, all of her thoughts were whirling around in her head.

"Come on Storm, you can do it, girl." She bent low in the saddle, letting the mare go. She knew Titus had a fast horse too but she had faith that

Storm could get her away from the man closing in on her.

There was a ravine crossing the property up ahead, so she pulled Storm in a bit to make sure the mare wouldn't get hurt as she jumped across. As they approached it, she suddenly felt the horse move sideways as she tried to stop. Something had spooked her at the last minute and, before she could stop herself, Ella felt herself being flung from the mare's back through the air.

She closed her eyes and braced herself for the moment she hit the ground but she still wasn't prepared for the pain that shot through her hip as she landed square on a rock poking from the earth.

She skidded along the ground, her face being whipped by the small branches lining the edge of the ravine. As she lay for a moment to catch her breath, and to make sure she could still move everything, she cringed when she saw the shadow fall over her.

"Ella! Are you all right?" Titus leaped from his horse and was on his knees beside her.

She really didn't want to talk to him. She tried to sit up but pain shot through her hip as she moved. Wincing, she sucked in a breath and laid back down. She was stuck laying on the ground and had no option to get away from Titus.

But, she wasn't going to look at him.

She hit at his hands as he reached out to brush

the leaves and dirt from her face. "Leave me alone, Titus. I'm fine. I just need you to get away from me." She wouldn't open her eyes, determined not to look into the eyes she knew would be staring back at her.

The same eyes that seemed to have some kind of spell over her and she knew she wouldn't be able to think straight.

He didn't speak or move for what seemed like minutes, so she started to worry that he was up to something. She peeked one eye open to see what he was doing.

Against the orange of the sun, she saw him sitting on the ground simply watching her. "I'm not going anywhere until you talk to me, Ella, so you may as well open your eyes and get it over with."

She clenched her teeth together, frustration at not being able to get away from him taking hold of her. Once again, she moved to sit up, letting her eyes squeeze tight against the pain as she got herself upright.

"I've got nothing to say to you. You're nothing but a lying swine who took advantage of a situation so he could get his hands on all of the land. You're no better than Garett Jackson." She didn't really believe what she was saying but her heart was wounded and she needed to lash out at him.

Even though it was getting dark, she could make out the eyebrow he raised in her direction.

"For a woman who has nothing to say to me, you sure managed to fit a lot in."

She rolled her eyes and looked away from him. The sounds of the frogs in the water near the ravine reached her ears and the slight breeze in the air cooled her cheeks.

Titus reached his hand out and gently turned her face to him. This time, he held it firm and when she reached up to brush his hand away, he grabbed it with his free hand.

"No, Ella. You're going to look at me and you're going to listen. For once in your life, you're going to do as someone tells you." She glared at him through squinted eyes.

"Here you go, sweet talking me again."

This time, she was sure she saw him roll his eyes.

"Ella, I never told you about the land because it didn't matter. Walter and I had talked about it weeks before he was killed. He told me he wanted to leave me his land when he was gone but that he also wanted to make sure you were taken care of too. He knew he wasn't a young man anymore." He pulled his hat off and threw it to his side.

"I promised him that I would make sure you had everything you needed even if anyone tried to protest that a woman couldn't own land on her own. The laws are changing but some people are still behind the times and if anyone tried to argue against the will and say you didn't have the right to own the land, you could lose everything. My name is on the majority of the title for the land but I promised my uncle it would be yours."

He watched her carefully as his thumb started to caress her chin where he still held it facing him.

"I would never break that promise. I'd planned to go back home and just let you keep working the farm how you saw fit. I was going to tell you the truth but I knew, if I did, you'd just say you didn't need any charity and walk away from the life on this farm that I know you love."

She wanted to believe him.

He dropped his hand and looked down as he pushed it back through his hair. The day had taken its toll on both of them and she noticed his hair had dried in curls all around his face.

When he looked back up, he reached out and took her hand in his.

"I never planned to stay. I never planned to become invested in anything more than catching who had killed my brother and my uncle." She heard him swallow and let herself close her eyes as his thumb caressed her hand.

"And, I never planned to fall in love with the woman working on that farm, the woman who has given me more headaches than a man should have in a lifetime."

Her head started to spin and her eyes flew open.

His face was inches from hers and his eyes trapped her in the darkness.

"But..." This was the moment she'd dreamed of all her life. The man she loved telling her he loved her too. And, she couldn't think of anything to say.

He lifted his hand and pushed the hair back from her face, tucking some stray tendrils behind her ear.

"Ella, I want to stay. I want us to have a real marriage. It scares me more than I could ever admit, to think I might ever be able to hurt you like my father did to my ma, but I can't stand the thought of riding away and never getting to spend another day with you." His voice was husky with emotion and she realized how much of a burden he carried, worrying about being like his father.

She lifted her hand to touch his cheek and she heard him take a sharp intake of breath. The muscles in his jaw were working as he waited to hear what she'd say.

"Titus, you're nothing like your father. I've never felt afraid around you. You've shown more patience than most men I know and I see a side to you that lets me know the kind of man you truly are." She swallowed and took a breath before she continued.

"Besides, any man who could care for a flea-bitten old mule the way you have, could never be anything else but gentle." She smiled at him as she saw his eyebrow quirk again at the mention of Wally.

"You might not believe it about yourself but the man I've gotten to know is a man I know I could never live without. You might frustrate me, and make me angry more times a day than should be possible, but I know you've always been there when I needed someone to make me feel safe."

"Ella..." His voice came out as a groan as he put his hands up behind her head and pulled her toward him. When she felt his lips touch hers, she was sure her heart would explode right from her chest.

This was what she'd dreamed about. This was what her ma had told her it would feel like when she was with a man she loved.

His lips moved on hers hungrily and she felt him pulling her closer to his chest. She let out a whimper at the pain that shot through her side but held tightly so he wouldn't let her go.

His head pushed back and he looked down into her eyes. The darkness had engulfed them, but the moon shone brightly above their heads letting her see the yearning in his eyes. "I'm sorry, I didn't mean to hurt you."

She pulled his head back and gently touched his lips.

"Titus, you could never hurt me. I love you." She looked deep into his eyes as he held her close.

The sound of an animal snorting broke the spell

between them. Hooves could be heard making their way toward where they sat on the ground in each other's arms.

Titus leaned his forehead onto hers. "Wally." The word came out as a groan.

Ella laughed as she moved her head back and looked in the direction of the sound. She could see the mule making its way toward her, beside two figures on horses. She could see Logan had Garett's hands tied securely around the saddle.

"Poor old Wally's been back and forth all day. He should sleep good tonight." She had to smile at the animal as it came up and nudged her with its nose.

"Well, that's good because I don't want any interruptions when I get you home." Titus pulled her close as he pressed a quick kiss to her lips. Wally didn't want to be ignored, so he pushed himself into Titus until he had to pat him behind the ears.

Her brother rode up alongside them and looked down with a grin.

"Well, looks like you caught up to her, Titus." He moved his eyes to hers. "Everything all right, sis?"

She smiled up at him, then turned and took Titus's hand in hers.

"Everything is exactly how I'd always dreamed it could be."

EPILOGUE

Colton was grinning from ear to ear as he placed the wrapped bundle in Ella's arms. She looked down in wonder at this tiny face that looked up at her.

"His name is Robert, after our pa." Colton smiled down at the baby.

Phoebe's sister Grace walked over with another bundle and placed it Titus's arms. Ella laughed at the worried expression that filled his face as he carefully stood, scared to move with the baby he held to his chest.

"And, this is Laura, named after Phoebe's ma."

Colton was the perfect picture of proud father as he looked at the twins they were holding in their arms.

"Oh Phoebe, they are perfect." Ella looked down

with tears in her eyes at her sister-in-law who was already up and sitting in a chair.

Robert decided it was time to remind them all he was there and he let out a loud wail. Phoebe smiled up and reached out for the baby. "He's hungry again." Ella placed him back in his mother's arms, then turned to look at Titus.

He was smiling down at the tiny girl in his arms and she was reaching up and gripping his finger with her small hand.

Ella's heart squeezed with love as she looked at the man in front of her. They'd been through so much together, fighting for the farm that had belonged to the man they both loved. He'd never let her feel like she wasn't capable of working alongside him and had generously made sure he kept his promise to his uncle.

Her heart had never felt so full.

The door swung open and Logan came through with their mother right on his heels. Through the open doorway, she could see Audrey and Reid's wagon making its way up the lane. The Wallace family never missed a chance to get together and meeting the newest members of the family was a big occasion.

Garett had been taken to Oregon City to face the judge and Ella didn't even know what would happen to him. She didn't care. He'd let greed get the best of him and two innocent people they loved had lost their lives because of it.

Logan had bought the title to Garett's land, so now the Wallaces held the largest amount of land in the area. The gold mine ended up not producing as much gold as everyone had thought which made Ella's heart break even more at the lives lost over something that wasn't worth more than the land itself.

Reaching out, she gently touched her niece's cheek. "She sure is beautiful." She whispered softly as the sounds of her family arriving reached her ears.

Titus lifted his hand and touched her cheek. "She must get it from you." She rolled her eyes, then playfully tapped him on the arm. He knew she was uncomfortable when he paid her compliments.

"My turn!" Audrey had come through the door and was already lifting Laura out of Titus's arms while Robert was fed. The sound of everyone talking and laughing together warmed her heart.

But, she wanted to be alone with Titus. She smiled at him, then took his hand and tilted her head toward the doorway.

He took the hint and smiled back, following her out onto the porch.

They walked in silence for a few moments listening to the sounds of the birds singing in the trees and the quiet trickling of the creek that ran by the house. She leaned in and laid her head on Titus's shoulder, wrapping her arms around his arm.

"Thank you." She knew it sounded strange to be thanking this man who was her husband but she was having trouble finding the words she was feeling in her heart.

He pulled back and looked down at her with his eyebrows creased together.

"For what?"

She just smiled to herself. "For being exactly the man I needed and for making me so happy."

Titus gave a little laugh. "I reckon I'm the one who should be thanking you."

She turned and let his arms go around her waist as she put her own onto his shoulders.

"I always dreamed of marrying for love and I'd given up on that ever happening. I dreamed of having a home of my own and now I have one with you."

She was having a hard time remembering what she wanted to say as his fingers rubbed along her back, leaving a trail of heat even through the fabric of her blouse.

"And, I'd always dreamed of having my own family, with my own children on my knee, and now you've given me that too." She waited as the confused expression on his face turned to disbelief.

"You mean..." She nodded her head.

"I'm going to have a baby."

She squealed as Titus lifted her in the air and swung her around, her long skirt flowing around behind her.

"What's going on?" Logan was the first one out on the porch at the sound of his sister's scream. He looked all around to see what the danger was.

"We're having a baby!" Titus's voice reached the ears of everyone who'd followed the sound outside and, within seconds, they were pushed apart by the family congratulating them and patting Titus on the back.

Her eyes found Titus and he was smiling back at her. She just shrugged, knowing what her family was like, and hoped he would get used to it too.

Wally came loping over from where he'd been laying in the shade of the porch. He came wherever they went when they visited family and sometimes even rode in the back of the wagon.

Titus still grumbled about the animal but Ella knew how much he genuinely cared about Wally.

"Old Wally here is going to be jealous." Reid reached down and patted him on the head.

Ella watched as Wally got into the middle of the group of people on the lawn, pushing his way toward Titus.

As she stood watching the people in front of her, hugging and laughing, her eyes found Titus's again. He pushed his way through the crowd and came over to take her hands in his.

"Thank you, Ella, for believing I could be a man worthy of your love."

He bent down and kissed her so tenderly she was sure her legs would give out. When he lifted his head, she tilted her head to the side as she touched her fingers to his cheek.

"Do you suppose Walter would be happy to know we found each other?"

He smiled down at her.

"I have no doubt that Walter knew what he was doing when he left this land to the two of us. He was an old softy who believed in love but he knew I'd never let myself find it. He knew you'd be the only one who wouldn't give up on me."

She pulled him close and rested her head on his chest, listening to the sound of his heart beating.

She whispered softly to herself, hoping he could hear her. *Thank you Walter, for making sure I had my dream come true.*

TAKE A LOOK AT BOOK FOUR:
HOPE'S HONOR

Left in the care of her vindictive stepmother after the death of her father, Hope is shocked to find out the debt he's left them in. However, that's nothing compared to the horror she feels when she finds out how her stepmother intends to pay off that debt without losing any of her luxuries. With a little brother who has been deaf since birth, Hope has no choice but to go along with it to protect him.

Logan Wallace has travelled to Sacramento to purchase the cattle he needs to start his own herd, only to be greeted by a pickpocket shortly after he arrives. Chasing the thief, he's led into the slums of the town where he's shocked to see some kind of human auction happening.

When his eyes meet the terrified brown ones

...ck at him from the wooden platform, he
...he can't walk away and leave her there to the
...of the men who are bidding.

Putting up the money he was supposed to use to
purchase a prized mare for his sister Ella, he steps in
to help. But when he wins the auction and tries to
let the girl have her freedom, he's shocked to find
out that her honor won't allow her to walk away
until she's paid him back in full.

So now what is he supposed to do with her?

AVAILABLE APRIL 2022

ABOUT THE AUTHOR

USA Today Bestselling Author, Kay P. Dawson writes sweet western romance – the kind that leaves out all of the juicy details and immerses you in a true, heartfelt love story. Growing up pretending she was Laura Ingalls, she's always had a love for the old west and pioneer times. She believes in true love, and finding your happy ever after.

Happily married mom of two girls, Kay has always taught her children to follow their dreams. And, after a breast cancer diagnosis at the age of 39, she realized it was time to take her own advice. She had always wanted to write a book, and she decided that the someday she was waiting for was now.

She writes western historical, contemporary and time travel romance that all transport the reader to a time or place where true love always finds a way.